JUNEBUG

Based on a true story

Cherie Doyen

Artwork by Emily Doyen

BALBOA
PRESS

A DIVISION OF HAY HOUSE

Interior Graphics/Art Credit: Emily Doyen

Balboa Press books may be ordered through booksellers or by contacting:

Balboa Press
A Division of Hay House
1663 Liberty Drive
Bloomington, IN 47403
www.balboapress.com
1-(877) 407-4847

Because of the dynamic nature of the Internet, any web addresses or links contained in this book may have changed since publication and may no longer be valid. The views expressed in this work are solely those of the author and do not necessarily reflect the views of the publisher, and the publisher hereby disclaims any responsibility for them.

The author of this book does not dispense medical advice or prescribe the use of any technique as a form of treatment for physical, emotional, or medical problems without the advice of a physician, either directly or indirectly. The intent of the author is only to offer information of a general nature to help you in your quest for emotional and spiritual well-being. In the event you use any of the information in this book for yourself, which is your constitutional right, the author and the publisher assume no responsibility for your actions.

Any people depicted in stock imagery provided by Thinkstock are models, and such images are being used for illustrative purposes only. Certain stock imagery © Thinkstock.

ISBN: 978-1-4525-7203-1 (sc)
ISBN: 978-1-4525-7205-5 (hc)
ISBN: 978-1-4525-7204-8 (e)

Library of Congress Control Number: 2013906415

Printed in the United States of America.

Balboa Press rev. date: 05/08/2013

I want to send out a wave of thanks to my husband, Steve, and all of those who stood by me through this process. Special thanks to my girls, Danielle and Emily and their Dad, Rob, who wove their expertise together flawlessly culminating in Junebug, a labor of love. From the limb of our tree...

Tree of family and relatives

My story begins in this sleepy little railroad town. It sits off the interstate in the foot hills. With no through traffic, the town hasn't had much influx of new people or new thoughts in decades. This is a town of secrets. From the outside, a cute little town that hasn't been touched much by change. The landscape is filled with rolling hills and streams. There's a creek, big enough to swim in, running right through town. Don't look too closely at the chipping paint and sagging porches. Everyone is related to everyone, a place no one ever leaves. A place where nothing is as it seems.

I live on a tiny little farm outside of town in a ramshackle house. I've lived there most of my life, except for a short stint in the city in the very beginning. The house is a constant work in progress. The family consists of me, two younger brothers and my parents...or so they say. I'm not sure. *Can I really be related to these people? Is it really their blood running through my veins?* The younger of my two brothers, Sam, seems to be on the outside too. He doesn't seem like the rest. I keep him very close at all times, for safety. I don't want them to be able to get to him, his mind. The middle boy, Kenny, is meaner than a snake. They've gotten to him already.

Our small piece of property is surrounded by a larger farm owned by Mr. Stanford. He has about a hundred acres. The old man has taken a shine to me and my love for animals. He has a beautiful Irish setter named Joe. I love the way his shiny red coat feels sliding through my fingers. Seeing the old man out in the pasture, tall, lean, walking stick in one hand, his faithful companion on the other, makes me smile from the inside. I'm off and running. I cover the distance between us as fast as my legs will carry me. If I'm lucky, we get to spend the day in the garden. He loves to teach me as we go along, telling me about each plant and what it needs to be healthy and strong. This is my favorite time, maybe because he feels I'm worth teaching. Whatever the day turns into, chores are always more fun when they're someone else's.

Mr. Stanford lets me graze my horse Ginger in his pasture. The grounds are mine to roam whenever I want, my playground. The beautiful hills and cliffs are my refuge. By the time I reach the creek, the grime from home is washed away and forgotten. For the moment freedom and laughter replace reality.

Celtic symbol for mother.... Mother is her nurturing state, maiden in her innocence, crone in her wise experience

Grandma, my angel. When I'm at Grandma's, all of Dad's stupid rules go right out the window. I'm not allowed to be held or rocked. *"Don't want some spoiled brat."* When I'm with Grandma I get all the love and touching I want. She holds me and rocks me, singing me her funny little songs. *How much is that doggie in the window?* She loves me and she loves me right. When I'm at Grandma's I'm the favorite. She can barely turn around without stepping on me. I always want to be on her lap; women sitting around the table gabbing, and there I am looking up longingly.

"Go play and leave Grandma alone for a while, now," Mom tells me.

"No, no she's all right," Grandma says, "Come here, sweet Junebug."

I climb up and cuddle in her arms.

The connection most people have with their mother, that's the connection I have with Grandma. Grandma and Mom all rolled into one. The problem is, I don't live here. I only get her sometimes. She isn't my Mom. My support and safety is once removed.

I have one memory of when I was quite small. I'm left in the driveway, in an old Rambler station wagon, while Mom goes in to talk to Grandma. I'm told to wait. I have on a little yellow dress and white hat; my feet don't reach the edge of the seat. I'm in the front seat, can't see out and afraid to move. After a few minutes, I hear the squeak of the old screen door and the swing of the gate. Mom opens the back door of the old car and takes a little suitcase from the back seat. She then crosses around the front, opens the passenger door, scoops me up and carts me inside. I wasn't sad being dropped off there. I got a little vacation. Only, after a few days of being there, the anxiety would start, as if they were calling me.

Why would you want to go back there? my brain yells. *It's safe here people don't hurt you, and you're the favorite.* In my gut there is the feeling that I have to get back home, to make sure things are okay. The battle inside increases, until I'm asking to go home. Maybe it's the feeling of being dropped off there to get me out of the house? That became Mom's way of fighting for me after a while—dropping me off at Grandma's. The separation gives us all a rest for a second. Even though I love being here, it is a weird feeling to know why.

Chinese symbol for father

My first memory of my Dad is far from a pleasant one. The three of us lived in the city for a short while at the beginning of my life. Times were hard on my Mom; she was moved away from her family. She hadn't ever really been anywhere, much less lived anywhere other than her sleepy little town. She was far away with no car. Her pride got in the way of admitting what life was really like with her new husband and baby. The baby cried all the time, especially if her Daddy was around. *Yes, I was already scared to death of him. They think kids don't remember things from this young of an age. I'm here to tell you they do.* One particular day Mom had gone out to run errands. She was allowed this luxury within an allotted amount of time, whatever he deemed appropriate for the task, a curfew of sorts. I was left alone with my Dad.

On cue, I begin to cry and when he enters my room, I begin to howl. He checks my diaper, and with his touch my cries grow louder and even more intense.

There's nothing to do but lift her and give her a little shake; see if that shuts her up. No, that didn't work. How about a good smack? What do you know? That didn't work either. What now? He lays me down and leaves the room. My howls are deafening at this point.

He shuts the door, pops a beer, and paces in circles around the tiny apartment, the cries wearing on his every nerve. *How long can she possibly last?* He's not able to bear it another moment—oh, wait, first another beer, that always helps—he then decides he's going to have to teach me a lesson. He lifts me from the crib saying, *"You better shut up if you know what's good for you."*

I didn't.

Another good shake…. More crying. A few more smacks. Finally, exhausted and in shock, I gasp for air. Then, the quiet. Only the heavy breathing from crying so hard, for so long. He leaves the room, proud of himself.

Mom returns right on time. "I taught that screaming kid a lesson", he tells her, gloating,

"Finally got her to shut up. You just have her spoiled rotten."

She quickly takes the few steps to the baby's room. She's horrified. The bruises are already beginning to appear on her little baby's body, and she's quiet, eerily quiet. Tears stream down Mom's face. Holding me in close to her body, she makes a beeline for the door. If she can just get to the door, maybe she can get to the neighbors.

She never made it.

Screaming, hitting, crying. She was still fighting for me then.

The settlement was to move back home, back to the safety and comfort of her family. Of course, there were promises of no more hitting. I watched this from my safe spot, in the corner from above. I watched it all. It was before I was called to the other place. I was about six months old at the time. *We remember. Eventually we always remember.*

Chinese symbol for younger brother

The boys and I are all three years and some months apart. I'm the oldest, then Kenny…Sam's the baby and my pride and joy. I feel as if I have birthed him myself. He is so weak and so tiny. My goal is for him to be a kid, to believe in fairy tales, Santa Claus, and the Easter bunny. I want him to have the part of life I'm missing, the magic. He had a hard time in the beginning and had to stay in the hospital for a really long time after he was born. The waiting: it was bad enough to wait that whole time he was in her belly, but now this. She's back home, and he has to stay there all by himself, and here we are like nothing's happening. It feels like it's never going to end. Then finally the day comes when they get to bring him home. There is no sleeping the night before. I have been waiting for so long. The crib was set up outside my parents' room, in a little alcove. I'm not allowed to go with them into the city to the hospital, so I wait, and wait, and wait. Grandma does her best to keep me distracted, but I can't pay attention to her stories today. I hear the tires on the gravel drive and bolt from the house. I'm about to pee my pants I'm so excited. Mom has him pulled in close to her chest.

"Wait, I can't see."

I have to be patient until they get him inside, I'm told. More waiting. It's like Christmas, the anticipation and all the waiting. After getting settled inside, the blankets are pulled away, and I finally get a look at him. I'm stunned, speechless. He's the scrawniest, ugliest little thing I have ever seen. He kind of looks like an alien…boney head, big eyes and really skinny body.

My attention turns to my mother's voice as she explains to Grandma, "They won't know about his brain function until he's older. It could go one way or the other, either genius IQ or learning disabilities. They just don't know."

My heart begins to grow with compassion for the pitiful looking little thing. I decide then and there that he's going to be just fine. I kneel by his crib through the night praying. I promise God that I will keep Sam safe if He'll let this funny little creature be okay. Mom finds me in the morning, still perched on the stool, knees swollen. I'm stuck between the rails of the crib. It takes a pretty good size jar of Vaseline to get me free.

Before long I began to see the results of my prayers. The little thing begins to grow stronger. I hold true to my word, try to anyway. The boy is rarely out of my sight. He is a ball of light. Once he finally gets going, he never stops moving and he never stops talking. By age three or four he has bleeding ulcers. He's never touched. He's a sensitive boy. I can't protect him from the feelings. With my prayers answered, I have a job to do.

Kenny and I had it the toughest. Now Kenny's a big boy. He passed me up by about the age of five. Dad worked hard to make a mini-me out of Kenny. They even have the same name. I can remember Dad giving him sips of beer as a toddler just to watch him stumble around. He thought it was hilarious. It didn't seem too funny to me. Everyone would chuckle, watching. He was just a little boy. I guess it was one of the many battles Mom decided not to fight. Kenny was taught that if someone hurt you, you hurt them back and hurt them worse. The accident part was left out. If Kenny got hurt, someone paid. He was a very handsome little boy, with a smile that sparkled…in the beginning.

Kenny rarely spoke. He didn't say a word until he was three years old. Everyone thought something was the matter with him. He just didn't have anything to say. He watched. When he finally spoke, it came out in complete sentences. He was taught that women were stupid, and that included Mom. He challenged her at every turn, in his silence. He appeared to listen while doing whatever he wanted. I remember one time—Mom's after him about something and asks him if he wants a spanking, His reply, "*Well if it'll make you feel better.*" They had little, if any, expectation for Kenny. He could have F's and D's without a word, while I'll be in trouble over a B. I noticed a look that would enter his eyes. I think he did it on purpose just to see if anyone cared. They didn't. More fuel for his fire.

Dad got him sweet on the liquid gold with all those sips. They would head out to cut firewood with a twelve pack, well before Kenny was old enough to drive.

Dad wanted Kenny to be tough. He enrolled him in boxing. Kenny wasn't mean on the inside. He just had to act like it. He didn't really like hitting people; he was made to. I guess it became a way of life. By high school he was smoking, drinking and fighting. The boy everyone was afraid of—following right in Daddy's footsteps. "Mini-me" accomplished.

By the time he was thirteen, he and Dad were about the same size. Then the games really started. The rest of his time there, Dad spent making him feel little. It was hard to watch, really hard to stand by and watch someone get hurt.

We only had one television, until Kenny got one. Dad put an old television in Kenny's room on the wall that we share. He was allowed to keep it on all night....

Kenny would try and coach me on being invisible. He had it down. *Stay out of his way and be quiet. Stay close to the edges of the room and stop talking. Stop with the questions.* It was the talking part I never could seem to master. It didn't seem to matter anyway. Kenny knew; Dad was just waiting.

Tree of family and relatives

My two best friends, here, were Ginger and my little dog Chi-Chi. Ginger's original owner purchased a fox trotting mare with foal. The mare had bred with a quarter horse, which made the foal worthless…to them. I fell in love; we were a perfect match, both out of the loop. She had just been weaned from her mother when she came to live with us. She has this beautiful apricot coat with a crooked white blaze down her nose. I got to name her. I don't care what they say, she's perfect and worth everything to me. We've grown up together.

My friend Chi-Chi was acquired through a trade. Much to my poor little brother Sam's horror, Dad left that morning with his pony and came home with a Chihuahua. While loading the pony in the trailer, Dad explained to Sam that he was trading his pony for a dog. Sam had in his head a dog—a real dog of his very own, one that he could run and play with. He was so excited.

Hours later, here comes Dad, trailer empty. We meet him in the drive, all four piled around the cab of the truck waiting. He can't get out fast enough. He's already chuckling, anticipating the look on Sam's face.

Sam impatiently asks, "Where's my dog?"

Dad points to his shirt pocket. Laughing, he takes this teeny-little-thing from his pocket and holds her out to Sam. "She rode the whole way home, right here in my pocket," Dad says, patting his chest.

Sam looks at her in total disbelief, the tears welling up in his eyes. "You traded my pony for that? You said a dog."

The tiny creature fits in the palm of my father's hand. Dad is explaining, "When she gets all grown up, she is only gonna be about three pounds."

At this point, Sam's tears begin in earnest. "How could you leave with my pony and come home with a mouse?"

I feel sorry for him but intrigued at the same time by the tiny little creature.

"This little thing is worth a hell of a lot more than that pony," Dad tells him.

Sam doesn't care about that. All he knows is his pony was traded for a puppy no bigger than a mouse. Storming off to his room, Sam feels totally betrayed.

For me it's love at first sight. She's so tiny, "Can I hold her?"

Handing her to me, Dad talks about breeding her. *How could something this small have babies? Three pounds?* I can feel her tiny heart beat in the palm of my hand. I nuzzle her to my cheek. She's perfect. Chi-Chi becomes my baby. I carry that little dog everywhere. Wherever Ginger and I go, she goes. The three of us become inseparable.

Rangoli is a symbol from India....
It reminds us to not value the works of man
and possessions over God and the world
of the spirits

Until high school, I went to a small Catholic school right up
the street from Grandma's. It was perfect, my not being so
good with people and all. I went to school with the same
twenty five kids through the eighth grade. We went to church every
morning and confession every Friday afternoon. Church twice on
Friday, counting confession. The only day I didn't go to church was
Saturday. The school was situated next to the grand old church. We
were marched to church each morning in a line taking our places in
the pews, little kids in the front. We were seated according to grade.
The church was magnificent. I would lose myself in the paintings of
the angels and stars on the ceilings, everything trimmed out in gold.
The priest would stand with his back to us, uttering words in Latin
that no one could understand.

On confession day, I would sit waiting for my turn to go into the little closet to tell the priest my sins for the past week. I would think and think, knowing I did terrible things. Dad thought so, anyway. I just couldn't remember what they were. So I would conjure up something and hope the Hail Mary's would help me stay out of trouble.

I never quite understood the God they spoke of. I didn't understand about the babies and the baptism thing. It had me stumped. Why would God create a baby then decide if the parents' didn't pour water over its head, it should be thrown away? Eternity in hell? *I'm not sure parents should have that much power. They have enough already.* Anyway, made no sense to me. The nuns were always very patient with my constant stream of questions.

It seemed no one saw the layers, all the behind the scenes stuff. God doesn't have layers, does He? Like, what about the priest who was fooling around with all the old rich ladies, driving around in his fancy car? He thought no one knew. Or the one who seemed good but different. Some talked that he was gay. I didn't know what that meant. I liked him well enough; he was just a little different. Didn't matter; so was I.

Father Eddie was a dear friend of my Grandma's. He was one of the good guys, one of the few men I could trust. I loved him. Grandma did a lot of talking to get me and my brothers in school there. Dad was not going to pay for school. Father let us go for free. He'd pull me from class and carry me around the school on his shoulder while he did his rounds. I was his little fluff muffin. I would go back to class feeling a little puffed up and important. He wasn't so nice to all the kids, though. He had quite a temper, but it never turned my way.

Uncle John is six years older than me. He went to school with me when I was really little. He was always upstairs. It made me feel better knowing he was there. Sometimes I'd catch sight of him when he was running errands. If I was lucky, we would end up out at recess together. He would often make a point of coming over and seeing how I was doing; if I was lucky I got a full blown hug. He was pretty cute and real popular. I felt pretty special with all the girls drooling, wishing they were me…at least for a second.

Guardian angel

When I was in the second grade, the teacher was late one day. All twenty-five kids are locked out in the hall. Everyone's talking about their night before. These situations are hard. I never know what to talk to other people about. Early on, I learn it gets pretty awkward when I talk about what happened at my house last night. So I keep quiet. Class has begun for everyone else. One of my closest people friends, Sally, notices my barrette and gets the bright idea that we should pick the lock. The rest of the kids think it's a pretty good idea too, so they all chime in.

"Come on. Do it. They do it in the movies all the time."

"Oh come on. We're tired of standing out here."

"I want to go in!"

I'm thinking, not so smart, but maybe, if I do this, they'll like me and we'll have something fun to talk about. After lots of convincing, I take the barrette from my hair and begin the process of picking the lock. Of course, the barrette breaks off. While I'm struggling to get it out, our teacher shows up. Everyone plays dumb.

"June did it," they say, throwing me directly under the bus.

Luckily the door has a window above it, one of those transom things. She calls for the janitor, hoping to get someone to climb through and open it from the other side. It doesn't take long for them to decide that a grown man can't fit through the window. A decision is made: send for one of the older boys from upstairs. Guess who they send down? The smallest boy in the eighth grade...my Uncle John. I take off running. How humiliating! Uncle John?? This can't be happening. I lock myself in a stall in the bathroom and won't come out.

Standing outside the door Mrs. Evans talks and talks, trying to reassure me. "You're not in trouble, June. I think you've already learned your lesson. No punishment could be worse than what you're doing to yourself. No one's perfect. Everything has worked out just fine. Come on back to class now." She gets nothing in return but silence from the other side of the door, "We aren't going to tell your parents, June."

"John knows."

"Yes but we talked. This is going to stay between us. John isn't going to say anything to anyone."

I open the door a little, to peek out. "What about Grandma? She'll be so disappointed in me."

Mrs. Evans seizes the opportunity. She pulls the door open and scoops me into her arms. "It's okay now, let's go back to class."

"I can't."

"You have to come back sometime." She brought me back to the classroom holding my hand. She must have spoken to the class because no one said a word. John never mentioned it on the walk to Grandma's after school, not a word. He held true. I felt as if I had slid past that one.

The Triquetra is a Celtic symbol
representing a woman's life cycle...
maiden, mother, wise woman

Almost immediately upon the conception of my oldest daughter the flashbacks started. My mind had been blank of any memories of childhood. I was, by all accounts, Miss Happy-Go-Lucky, as if I had amnesia. I lived in the moment with no thoughts of the past, except for the constant underlying nagging to remember. Remember what?

Then the pictures started. Flashes of terror. Flashes of pain. Near death. With this new life growing inside, I felt the contrast between what I had versus what should be—the desire for joy, versus pain, for my little one.... Safety. *I need to know what happened to me so I don't make the same mistakes. I can't have her getting hurt.* I become consumed with the need to protect this precious life growing inside. *Can I do this? How can I be a mother? What do I do with all these pictures?*

No one around me notices the cracks that are appearing, severing my reality. Which side is true? This movie that I have been living has the feeling of missing scenes. Am I crazy? Dad's real reason for leaving the army is always floating around. He has that "crazy paper".

If he is really my father maybe I'm crazy too. Maybe this is how it starts. I just need to act normal, to blend in. Talking about it seems to make everyone uncomfortable, so I try and keep quiet. Everything around me is a likely trigger. Living with a man. Trying to be a wife. Sex. Now I'm a mother!

The black panther as an American Indian totem may symbolize an awakening to a heroic quest

I remember my mother giving me a bath. We were in the tiny bathroom, Mom on her knees beside the chipped porcelain tub. I remember the awkwardness of the moment. It wasn't customary to be touched much. There were about two or three inches of water in the tub. *Wouldn't want to be wasteful.* I tilt back as she pours the water over my head to rinse out the shampoo. The water filters down over my face. Her hands feel foreign as they skim my body. I'm pretty young. Mom wanted out of these sorts of interactions as early as possible.

I lie back, saying, "I wish I could slide down the drain with the water." I had no desire to die, just not to be here, in this place, in this body. I just wanted to be able to be free and go back to where I came from—the place before here, before this body, before these people.

Mom's response is immediate. "Don't you ever say anything like that again."

I just look at her. Lying there I get very still, very quiet. She pulls the stopper and the water begins to drain. I shut my eyes. I can feel myself being released from the confines of my body and this place they call my home. As the water begins to swirl around the drain, I can feel myself being pulled with the flow. I have the feeling of being afraid and peaceful at the same time. I notice the buildup of minerals on the pipes around me as I am carried along swiftly with the current, up and down. Twisting and turning until things begin to slow down a little. Suddenly, as if being poured from a faucet, I'm on solid ground, in a puddle. Standing, I shake myself off and look around. I'm a bit disoriented from the ride. The sun is shining brightly above the meadow I find myself deposited in. High above the grasses are flowers of all colors. A path runs along its edge. It doesn't look too different from home. It feels different though, or is it me who feels different? I must be dreaming. No, wait, I wasn't sleeping. I was getting a bath.

I look myself over thinking, *Am I gonna be able to get back?* Maybe I won't want to go back. A good way up the path I notice some movement. My first instinct is to run and hide, but running isn't smart. I know that much. Whatever it is could cover this distance in the time it would take for me to turn around. It looks like a cat. A really big cat. Slowly, I make my way into the grasses and crouch down low amidst the wild flowers. If it catches wind of me, that'll be it. It's coming right this way. In only seconds it is close enough to touch.

I sit, not moving a muscle, trying hard not to even breathe. He's standing there in all of his grandeur with long lean muscles, blue-black coat, and those eyes...the most mesmerizing yellowish green eyes you can imagine. Our eyes meet, and there I am face to face with a ginormous black panther.

His eyes, they're so captivating and kind. "It's okay, June," he says. "I'm not going to hurt you."

What? I have to be dreaming. I need to wake up now. Why can't I wake up? He's talking out loud, not in my head like back home. His voice has a velvety quality to it, the kind that makes you want to melt and instantly puts you at ease. Pulling from my toes, I gather every ounce of courage I can muster and push myself to my feet.

"It's okay, June," he says.

"Where am I?"

"You are safe here," he says.

"But where am I?"

"You will know soon enough," he replies.

As I look around I see there's no one else in sight. I have no choice but to trust him. "How do you know my name?"

"I have always known you; we have spent many lives together. We have had many adventures and fought great battles for the Teacher. It's time for another."

"Wait, fought great battles? I don't remember any battles, and... who's the Teacher?" My mind is searching for answers.

"You will remember when it's time," he says with a finality that tells me this part of the conversation is over.

"What about the Teacher?" I'm thinking he might know where I am and how I got here. He might even know how to get back...if I want to go back. "Grandma is going to be worried about me." Mom might be relieved though. It would be easier there, without me.

"You will know all, when it's time," is all he says.

After a moment or two of silence, "What's your name?"

"Tigua."

"Tigua; that's cool. What does it mean?"

"I was named after an Indian tribe that lives across the river," he says.

"Really? There are Indians here? I love stories about the Indians." I forget for a minute that I'm afraid. "Will I get to meet one, a real Indian, I mean?"

"All in due time, June, all in due time." Under his breath, through a low chuckle he mutters, "Some things never change."

What does he mean by that? I decide I should probably keep that question to myself.

"I need to take you to the Teacher. We don't have much time. Follow me."

"What do you mean, not much time?" I join him on the path. "I'm not sure I want to go back."

"Enough questions for now, June. The Teacher will have the answers you need." With that we fall into a silence. As I look around, I begin to take note of my surroundings, in case I need to find my way back by myself. The path runs along the meadow for a while. On the left is a boulder that looks like it has steps going up one side. *That'll be easy to remember.* The meadow eventually fades into a grove of trees. *Okay, got that.* To the right is a field of lush grasses that goes on as far as I can see. I hear the familiar sound of running water, *or is it draining water*?

He comes to a stop under a grand old tree laden with limbs bending to the ground under their own weight. I love trees almost as much as I love animals. He tells me to wait for the Teacher. He turns back gracefully in the direction we have just come.

"Wait," I call after him. I feel a little panic begin to creep in. "Don't just leave me here. What if he doesn't come?"

As he looks back over his shoulder, Tigua says with a smile, "He called you here June; He will come."

I watch anxiously as he disappears from view. Turning back towards the tree, I'm startled to see a man approaching. His long white robes flow with his stride. There's nothing to do but wait, I suppose. As he nears, I can see that he has a very kind face. He has a beautiful peaceful glow about him and some sort of familiarity that I can't quite place. It's as if I've always known him. I begin to relax, his peace seeming to calm me almost instantly. "Where am I?"

"You came here through the water, June. It's the water of life. This is a place where you can come to rest. A place where no one will harm you. Here you are protected always. Tigua will walk beside you, in this world and in the other."

"Oh, I'm not going back there," I tell him firmly.

"You must. You have things to do, things to learn, things to remember."

"I don't belong there; those aren't my people. They can't be. Nothing makes sense there."

"You are there to set things in motion. Sometimes life has to blow apart to allow for change. The women in your lineage have suffered greatly at the hands of men. You have to stop it. Only you can."

"I'm just a little girl, what can I do? He's so much bigger than me and he hurts me."

"I know. You have to understand the pain of all who have come before you. In experiencing, you will know, and gain the courage to stop it for all, giving peace to those who have come before you and freedom to those who come after. With each experience comes a tool of truth to add to your medicine pouch."

"Medicine pouch?"

"Yes, you are gathering tools for life and how to live it. In time, your pouch will grow full with wisdom and truth."

I can feel my eyes getting heavier with each word. *Wait. What is happening?* The scene is fading.

As I open my eyes, I'm back in the dark tiny oppressive bathroom, with the woman who claims to be my mother. She is urging me to get out of the tub and dry off. How can this be? It is as if no time has passed. She doesn't even know I was gone. I take a look around the room. I see the lonely light bulb hanging from the ceiling, the cold water knob still missing from the sink; the rusty pliers lying on the counter; the chipped, broken tiles. Yes, I'm back…. Home. I feel myself rise up to climb from the tub. *Was I just dreaming? What was that? It felt so real, somehow. I feel a little stronger, even if it was a dream. In dreams you don't feel, do you?* I can still feel his glow, Tigua's soft sleek coat between my fingers, the fear I felt well up at the first sight of him. I can feel the sun on my skin and the smell of the flowers. I'm brought back to reality with Mom telling me to get ready for bed as she finishes drying me off. I climb into my pajamas quickly and scurry off to bed in hopes of continuing my dream. As I drift off to sleep I can hear the customary fighting. I try to tune it out, but as always, it's about me.

Always fighting about me.

Tree of family and relatives

We did have some fun times, especially in the beginning. Dad worked the midnight shift at Chrysler, so by three in the afternoon, he was leaving for work. When school was in session, that meant he was already gone when we got off the bus. We only saw him on the weekends. During the summer, we tried really hard to avoid him. Mom had a lighter air about her then, too. We were all able to let down a little bit through the week. Mom and I were a team then. On the weekends, when things got ugly, it would be Mom and me against him. I'm not sure when or what changed that, what made her fade from view.

Mom's only sister, Carol, had two little boys. The boys, all within a few years of each other, got along famously. We had lots of adventures. Sometimes I was allowed to bring a friend, a people-friend, being the only girl. We couldn't spend any money because then Dad would know. My Mom's motto was: *"The more kids the better."* The kids could play and the grownups could visit. Sometimes, Grandma would join us with whatever crew she had at the time.

On those times, I would have to be forced to go play. Grandma's shadow. We'd all meet at the park for a picnic and play all afternoon. Grandma's contribution was always a great big watermelon for dessert. She loved watermelon.

The park has a wonderful creek that flows through the center. They would fish or catch crawdads. I didn't like the idea of catching either, so I always found something else to do. On crawdad days, the women and children would spend hours slowly lifting the rocks, in aim with their forks. They would stab the creepy little creatures with their forks and deposit them in the bucket. It made me sick to my stomach. After filling the bucket to their satisfaction, we would hurry up to Grandma's and cook them up. The women chattered while doing what they do, me, really not sure. I couldn't be talked into participating. I preferred a nice spot on the porch swing, listening to the commotion. From water, to bucket, to mouth...I stayed out of it. Always having a book tucked in my bag, I would be found curled up on the porch lost in my latest adventure when all was said and done.

Dollar movie nights at the drive-in were always lots of fun. Mom would load as many kids in the old station wagon as would fit, along with a cooler of food and sodas. We would pop our own popcorn and set up the lawn chairs next to another car full. Everyone knew everyone. The drive-in even had a playground. We were always there plenty early, so we could all play for awhile first. Friends would congregate around one car or another, kids running in all directions.

The Chat Dumps was another fun adventure. That was "a plan in advance day." It took a couple of hours to get there. Lunch prepared in a basket was put in the back, and we were on our way. The dumps were these enormous piles of a sand–like substance that looked like mountains. We would bring sleds, drag them to the top and ride at top speed down to the bottom. The climb to the top was agony, but coming down was a blast. It took forever to get the sand out of our hair.

Some evenings we would sneakily curl up in front of the television to watch Tom Jones, hoping we wouldn't get caught. We weren't allowed if Dad was home. He didn't like the way Mom looked at him. Vulgar! The rest of the world must have agreed because before long you could only see Tom from the waist up. That took all the fun out of it. The man could dance.

We would clean house to Elvis music blaring. We'd stop on Mom's favorite songs. She would grab my hand and give me a spin. Mom loved to dance, and she was good at it. The jitterbug was always her specialty. When I was a little girl, I had lots of fantasies about Elvis. What if I could have a dad like Elvis? I would dream of him tucking me in at night while singing to me softly, lulling me off to sleep. I was sure he would never, ever hit me. For sure, never the other things.

When the weekends came, everyone walked on egg shells, never knowing what would set off the inevitable explosion. Mom stood by me then. Us against him. She would fly in to my rescue and grab me up tight, as he ranted and raved, throwing things, breaking things....

That is if she got there in time. If I was already in his grip, she jumped in. I'm not sure why or when that shifted. Soon, I'd be left on my own in the battles. Where did she go?

Chinese symbol for Father

I'm not sure when Dad started slipping into my room. My memories are like Swiss cheese. I remember him sitting on the side of my bed...kissing...his tongue...standing at the edge of my bed...lurking around the bathroom.

The one bad thing about going to "the other place" is that I'm not here for things that are happening in my real life. On one hand, that's a good thing. The bad part is knowing something is happening but only having snap shots. How can I ever tell anyone, with only fragments? I'm left only with the feeling of terror. What I remember, I watched from above. When I don't want to watch anymore, I go on to the other place. Tigua is always waiting. Sometimes Grandma's there. I remember the first time I saw her.

*He encourages us to gain power from the
darkness no matter the depth of degradation,
with the promise of leading us back to the light*

I am met by Tigua. We begin meandering down the trail towards my beloved tree. I always get to see the Teacher at the tree. I'm running around the meadow picking flowers to bring to him. As I look up, I see a woman on the path up ahead. She's dressed in long white robes with a long red scarf draped from her head to the ground. She's waiting patiently for us to approach. I look her over very closely as I stand before her. She feels familiar somehow, but not her face. She feels comfortable as if I've always known her. Her gaze is soft and full of love. As I'm looking into her eyes, just getting close to the realization, the woman pulls me in close.

"Junebug!"

"Grandma!" No wonder she feels so familiar. No one calls me Junebug but Grandma, even here. My mind's popping with lots and lots of questions.

"Why are you here, Grandma? Why do you look so different?"

"All people have many faces and have lived many different lives. Our bodies are kind of like costumes for a play. When the time comes for the next play, you have to put on a different costume. Do you understand?"

I nod my head yes.

"Now, I have called you here today, June, so we can talk. So we can talk about the things that aren't talked about."

"He hurts me, Grandma." Taking me by the hand, she guides me to a nice soft spot in the meadow. We settle in amidst the flowers. Tigua's purr is soothing as he curls in beside me.

"He slips into my room at night and makes me do some...not very nice things."

The woman gently puts her arm around me and pulls me in closer; the embrace feels warm and comforting. "I know things that feel ugly are happening to you back home. And I know it doesn't feel fair. I am so sorry. Life is just one big school, and all these things that you are learning right now are going to give you the capacity to help people understand. With your experience of the pain, you will be joining the army, to raise the bar. Raising the bar for all children. You're going to help change things, Junebug."

I have no idea what she's talking about. All I know is that I'm made to do some really nasty things and I don't like it one bit. I sit in silence.

"How can I change anything? I'm just a little girl."

"You won't always be a little girl. Someday you will be all grown up with girls of your own, and you are going to know. They will be the first ones from our line to be free. You will know how to keep them safe. You will have enough tools to teach them to be strong women. Someday, you can use your knowledge to help others see, to see the web of pain that their mindless acts leave behind. You will remember. Your children will be safe. From here, the karma will be broken; our lineage will be free."

It made me uncomfortable somehow to leave my other part stuck in the crazy, down there, and the constant nagging of the missing memories.

It's as if the woman can read my thoughts.

"The missing pictures are not important to you now, Junebug. You have the memories; they are just in your knowing. The pictures you have now are enough. In time, they will become complete— when you're ready."

"I seem to leave before things get too ugly. I can remember for a while, until I leave the room to come here. Then I can't remember anything until after I get back."

"I know," Grandma says, as she strokes my hair. "You don't worry about that now. When you need the pictures and they are of use to you, they will come. Now they will only complicate things. Take what God has given you." She spread her arms wide, gesturing the length of the meadow. "Run, play, be free, without worry. You have plenty of time for worry at home. I want you to know that we can always talk from this place, June. Even down there. We can talk without words. I always know, Junebug, and I always care. You have a lot of people on this side looking out for you. We won't allow anything to harm who you are."

"He is, though, Grandma."

"No, no he's not. He can only affect you down there, in that world. Down there is only for learning. Down there is the game. You are learning so many things about strength and character. Lots of tools and truths are going into your medicine pouch, which means there are a lot of things that you are going to be able to affect. He's not winning, and we aren't going to let him. You are a survivor, a survivor of many battles with more yet to come. Never a victim, Junebug. Warriors are never victims; they choose to fight."

With that, I was back in my bed, with Dad padding out of my room.

Just as a spider weaves its web, we weave
our lives with our actions and our choices

I try to remember when Mom began fading from view. Was it before or after he started slipping into my room? *Why does she keep us here?* **Little girls need their daddies.** *I'm not at all sure I need this one. Is this what daddies are supposed to be like?*

She is sitting there, with her elbows on the table, head in her hands, as if she has given up, crying. My youngest brother hasn't made it here yet, so it is just me, Mom, and Kenny. I come up with a plan. I approach her, my little fingers grip the edge of the table. I'm up on my tip toes. I peer over the edge.

"Mom, can we please just go to Grandma's? She has that little room in the back and you know I can share with Grandma...."

"We can't go to Grandma's," she snaps. "She doesn't have the money, and there's just not enough room." Under her breath she mumbles, "She never wanted me to marry him, anyway."

"That doesn't matter. She loves us. She would never turn us away. She'll help us figure something out," I plead with her.

"We can't go there," she says with finality. "I can't do that."

At that moment I understood that the, *I told you so's*, carried more weight than our safety and well-being. A pit formed in my stomach that was with me for the rest of my time there, a realization of her weakness and that I was on my own to survive…hell. We were there for the duration. She's too weak to save us.

I became increasingly aware of the mental cage she lived in, how broken and beaten down she'd become. Dad was always accusing her of sleeping with somebody. One time, I remember there being quite a scuttle at a wedding reception because he had gotten it into his head that Mom and his own step-dad were making out on the dance floor. His jealousy was out of control. I felt sorry for her. Her spirit had been torn apart with his constant berating. After her childbearing came a barrage of insults about her body.

"Too stretched out' or **'Boobs look like two fried eggs"** these were only the things that were said in public, where little girls could hear. Lord only knows what was said behind closed doors. He actually went to the laundromat, timed the whole process, and came home with the framework for our trips. Same with the grocery. She had an allotted time for each. God help us if the washers were tied up, because there were no excuses. He would insist she must have met some guy up there…with three kids in tow. She was never allowed to go anywhere without us. She was given an allotted amount of money for groceries, nothing extra, with the expectation that the cabinets would be loaded to his satisfaction. No pocket change for her.

Mom's scarring was a constant point of ridicule. I never understood why. She was scarred from the beginning. They had been there when he met her. Why did they seem to bother him so much now? He definitely had a mean streak, saying things like, **"Look at you. Who else would have you? You would never get another man to even look at you."**

My mother had lived through a gas station explosion when she was sixteen. She was more than a little rebellious and angry at the time; she had just lost her father. They were really close. To hear Grandma tell it, Mom had him wrapped around her finger. She would get him up in the middle of the night for chocolate milk, and he would do it. He adored her. *I wonder if he visited her room at night.*

Mom and a girlfriend had been out cruising town. It was a beautiful summer day. The girls stopped in the gas station on the corner of Main Street to grab a coke and decided it might be smart to get one more bathroom break in first. They were meeting some friends for a day of horseback riding. The girls took a second to check their hair in the mirror to make sure they're looking good, since they were meeting boys there. Mom pulled a cigarette from her pack and as she lights her match…BOOM! The whole place went…POOF! The force of the explosion has the girls trapped in the bathroom. It felt like something was blocking the door, and she couldn't get it open. The room filled with smoke. Her friend turned into a heap on the floor, no help at all. As Mom struggled with the door her skin was melting. Finally, door free, Mom grabbed her friend and the two made their way out of the building. As they emerged from the flames, both girls were on fire, hair and all. The ambulance was waiting.

Her burns start at one ear and run most of the length of the front half of her body. Luckily, most of her face was spared.

She died twice on the table that day, as they were working to save her life. The first time she watched from above as the doctors worked. I guess she found a way out, too. The second time out she was met by her father before the light. He took her into his arms. She was so happy to see him.

She misses him so much.

"I know, but you can't stay here now. You have to go back."

She begins to cry. "No! I don't want to go back. It hurts so bad, Daddy. I can't do it."

"You have to; you have something very important to do, and only you can do it."

"Nooooo...." she cries as she's sucked back down into her body.

She was in the hospital for months and missed most of the coming school year. Her limits were reached with the possibility of having to have her left ear amputated. She just couldn't bear any more. The doctors explained that the ear was infected, and with the infection being so close to the brain, it was potentially really dangerous.

Mom pled, "Just one more day. It'll be better, I'm sure."

The doctors agreed they could postpone the surgery until the following morning.

Mother's nurse for the evening was a large black woman. Blacks and whites didn't mingle much in those days. In our sleepy little town, paths never crossed.

Laying a hand on my Grandmother's shoulder, the nurse asked, "Can I pray with you?"

Grandma's a little taken aback by the forwardness of the black stranger, but she couldn't turn down prayers, especially at a time like this.

"Please," is all she said.

While attaching a medal to the bandages on Mom's ear, the stranger whispers, "We are calling upon St. Jude, the Patron Saint of lost causes."

With that, the women went down on their knees, where they were found the following morning. As Mom was wheeled into surgery, her wails bellowed through the halls. Upon removing the bandages, they found the ear healed, free from infection. ***Completely*** *healed*. The doctors were astounded. No one ever saw the mysterious black woman with the powerful prayers again. Mom's angel.

Most are given the gift of life once; Mom received it three times.

Only to become invisible.

Maiden, mother, wise woman

A long came the first doctor. Mental help was totally taboo around here. People should be able to take care of their own stuff. But the new pictures that were taking over my head were so different from the stories told by the family. All I had were their stories versus my pictures. Dad didn't have the greatest disposition now…but this? How could this ever be rectified? This was not what Bob signed up for when we married. He knew what had been going on in the present. What he had witnessed and a little history. But a mental doctor? He was not at all convinced. Finally, we compromised, and Bob got me an appointment with one of the psychology professors at the college where he taught. I jumped on the guy's recommendation to confront them, the ones who claim to be my family, and tell them about the pictures.

Bob and I made the trip back home. The terror threatened to swallow me whole as we inched our way closer to the little town we used to call home.

Bob was a slight little man, and for some reason, the only person other than Grandma who got away with telling Dad to sit down and shut up, and he did it, every time. He sat right down, without a word. I remember the first time. We had been dating for a while and were planning to go on a trip out of town. I had almost made it out of the door, when Dad catches my arm. **Where in the hell do you think you're going?** Bob steps in and says to him,

"Now Kenny, we don't want any trouble. She's twenty-one years old. There's nothing that you can do, so why don't you just sit down there and be quiet." While he was talking I snuck out the door and locked myself in the car. I decided then and there I would follow him to the ends of the earth, and I did. I married him, and we moved to a city a few hours away where he would teach acting.

We have arranged for a meeting in the park. Bob and I have left our baby with Grandma. We get there first. I'm about to throw up. Bob's pacing. When the two that claim to be my parents arrive, Bob takes charge and arranges us around a picnic table. He puts on his booming actor voice and gives them both instructions to keep quiet until I finish what I have to say. Dad closes his mouth and stares down at the table. Mom looks me square in the eye with that **bring it on** look. So I did.

"I have these memories. They're just pictures. They come to me at night while I'm sleeping. I can't make sense of them. I need help. I need to know if they're true. I feel like I'm going crazy." The **crazy paper** is always in the back of my mind. Maybe I'm crazy just like him.

Lots of back crawling.

Eye contact is impossible at the moment. Finally staring at the table, Dad says, "I was a terrible father. I was a terrible person. Still am. I don't remember, but if you remember, I'm sure I did everything you say…I'm sorry."

Somehow, it fell flat. How was that going to help me? I need to put the pieces of the puzzle together, but there would be no help from him. He didn't even remember, or claims not to. How could he not remember his role in molding my life?

Mom just sits there. "Mom? Please? I need to know what happened to me. I have this aching feeling that some really horrible things have happened to me. In one of the flashes, I am just a little baby. It haunts me. I am still in a crib. I'm being jerked around; my head is bobbing back and forth. There is fear and then the quiet. I only get glimpses. Is it real? Please tell me."

Silence.

The scales signify a metaphysical sort of weighing, one side holds the conscience while the other holds the feather of truth

We went everywhere in hordes: Grandma, and whatever foster children she had at the time, plus aunts and uncles with a mess of cousins in tow. One beautiful sunny day we were going to the zoo. I have mixed emotions. I love seeing the animals, but I always leave the zoo sad. I can hear the animals' cries for freedom. They want me to help them. They know that I can hear them. What can I do? They long for their home lands. I know how they feel, being locked in a cage in a world that's not their own.

We are all loaded up. Dad has started out the day in good form. He loves these outings. It's bright and early. There's a picnic basket and cooler in the back, a fresh beer between his legs and a six pack on the seat between him and Mom: perfection. Charlie Pride is blaring on the radio. Kenny, Sam and I are crammed in the back in bucket seats, Sam and I together in one seat, because you don't touch Kenny. As usual, Sam never stops moving or talking. Talking and talking.

We finally get to the zoo, after the customary ten thousand, *"Are we there yets?"* from Sam, and pile out of the car. The air is full of chatter and excitement. Going into the city, in and of itself, is a special treat. Dad, always in charge, begins to herd us toward the gate. By this point, with three or four beers under his belt, he's good and happy. I say a little prayer that this is how he stays. I look back over my shoulder at the cooler, and I know that's not gonna be the case.

As we approach the gate, the chatter moves to where to go first. Everyone's talking at once. Finally, just as the kids are ready to explode, the grownups decide to split up in groups. We'll all meet back at the gate for lunch at noon. Grandma is coming with our group, thank goodness. We head in the direction of the elephants. I stick close to Grandma. *I never like being too far away or too close, at least arm's length. I have to keep a watchful eye in these sorts of situations.*

Standing in front of the elephants, the sadness comes. They want out of there. I can feel them, one in particular; she's calling out to me. She stood there swinging her leg in ultimate boredom. She misses her family, her free open space, her home. Through my gaze, I try to comfort her. Mom's tugging on my arm; everyone's ready to move on. I move away reluctantly, looking back over my shoulder. I don't want to break our connection.

Next stop is the reptile house. Kenny loves the snakes. I beg to wait outside. The snakes give me the heebie-jeebies. After some convincing, I'm placed on a bench under a beautiful tree while they tour the snake house. I can't get the elephant out of my mind. I wonder if any of the others hear them too, or if they just don't care. They don't seem to care about a lot of things.

Around lunch time, we all meet up and work our way through the gates back to the cars. The women stake out the perfect spot in a grove of trees and lay out the blankets for the kids. The men haul the coolers and picnic baskets over. The kids are loaded down with lawn chairs for the grown-ups, the ones with the metal frames and the striped woven straps. There's a nice breeze, so the coolers are strategically placed to hold the corners of the blankets down. The conversation is light and cheery. All of the food is spread out on a nearby picnic table. The boys are running and wrestling around. The girls are in a huddle, chattering…and then there's me on the fringe watching, waiting. By the looks of it, the beers are going down easy and the conversation is getting a little louder. *The tipping point is approaching.* After everyone is satiated, we do everything in reverse and work our way back inside.

The herd splits up again, heading in different directions, with a designated meeting time. Our group is aimed at the gorillas, Dad's pick. We stop and visit the exhibits along the way. The calling of the animals haunts me. Some just want to be heard; some are angry, some sad. A little bear cub, hanging from a little tree, reaches and cries out. He just needs a hug, too. I'm pulled away…destination gorillas.

I find myself standing in the presence of this huge ape. The beast is on the move, pacing in circles around the cage they call his home. His restlessness is thick and heavy. He's held in a cage with bars the size of Dad's arm. He has been given one lonely, dead tree; a rope hanging from the top of the cage, and a small pool of water. He's bored, and a little annoyed already. Then Dad starts in, as if fueled by the gorilla's unrest. I can feel the challenge mounting. I can almost imagine them circling each other, jungle style. I have witnessed this many times. Of course, typical of a bully, Dad can get away. He's going to win in the end, or so he thinks. *Get out of arm's reach; something's coming.* I find a place behind a bench and crouch down to watch the situation play out. The ape's agitation grows. Dad's throwing insults along with whatever he can find. The ape comes back with a splash of water. Dad hits him with a peanut. Debris flies

Dad's way. The ape's one up with a handful of poo. Dad dodges it. Now he's really pissed off. Mister Gorilla struts off and finds a place at the far corner of the cage. But Dad is just getting started. Here we go. The beast stands up to his full height, with his back facing us. He's acting cool, as if nothing's going on. He saunters over nonchalantly and plants himself right in front of the man who they say is my father. He takes aim and commences to relieve himself. It is like a fire hose. Dad's cursing and gasping. Everyone scatters in an attempt to hide their laughter as Mom tries to get the situation under control. She's yelling for someone to get some paper towels from the bathroom. In the mean time, she starts dabbing him off with napkins from her purse. I'm still hiding behind the bench out of sight, laughing so hard tears are rolling down my face. I catch a glimpse of Grandma. She's found herself a place off to the edge where she can enjoy the show, too. Our eyes meet as we're wiping the tears from our faces. She gives me a little wink, her eyes twinkling.

After the drama has played out to some degree, our family is gathered up because "We're getting out of this God damn place, away from that God damn stupid gorilla." In the car another beer between his legs, Dad curses the entire way, gagging between his swallows of liquid gold.

This is always the problem—going home. Fun is always tempered with—going home. At least this time, I have a good story. Whose dad gets peed on by a gorilla?

The key symbolizes opening and closing powers, possibly even secrets

As youngsters, we traveled from one house of cousins to another. I have two girl cousins. It wasn't long before I discovered that I wasn't alone carrying the keys to the locked up dark spaces.

I remember my eye level being just above the door knob. I hear some funny noises coming from behind the door that strike a weird nerve. I turn the knob ever so gently. Quiet as a mouse, I push the door open to Janet's room, just enough for me to see in. I see her older brother has her pinned down at the foot of the bed. She and I make eye contact. His pants are down around his feet, his manly parts inside her. His look tells me there will be all kinds of trouble if I talk. Her gaze implores me to close the door. I understand her reasons, and step back closing the door quietly.

Secrets. They're everywhere.

Junebug teaches us how to dig for answers to reveal your needed truths

The last day of school was always exciting. I enjoyed school; it was time away from the crazy, time where there was order, where you knew what was expected. But summertime, I loved summertime. The crew and I would explore the woods all day. We would climb up to our special spot, curl up with a book and lose hours. In the summer I can read whatever I want, whenever I want. I can go everywhere and be anywhere through the words on the page. Escape.

I get up bright and early, dress quickly, and off I go. I want to sneak out of the house. I try to beat the feeling of being forced out. By nine we're forced out, the door locked behind us, open again for lunch. This way it's my choice. The mind games we play with ourselves.

I creep through the house and open the door carefully. Once out in the open air, I breathe in. Freedom. Down to the barn I go. I use the word barn loosely; the barn is an old concrete block building. I imagine it being the original house. I had fantasies about the people that must have at one time lived their lives here. It has a front door with windows on either side and a little loft where we store the hay.

There's a door on the side that opens up to the feeding lot. We have no pasture, just woods. The feed is kept in an old freezer, the kind that opens from the top. Saw horses hold the saddles; bridles and halters hang from nails on the wall.

I scoop out the sweet corn and oat mixture and head out to give the horses their breakfast. All of the horses have been acquired through a trade or given to us. They are quite a mixture of beings, from a twenty-five-year-old Arabian to a poor stunted, malnourished filly. I have a soft spot for the filly. Her brain has been starved and she isn't quite right. The other horses don't have much to do with her. I try to make a special point each morning to spend some time with her and let her know someone loves her. The Arabian is Dad's mare. Unpredictable and aggressive, just like him. I have to be very cautious when I come out with the food; she would just as soon run me over as look at me. Back in to grab a bale of hay, throw the hose in the trough, and then the fun stuff. I love to climb into the loft while the horses are eating.

It's toward the end of summer, the loft's kind of empty. Baling time is just around the corner. I'm wandering around and stumble upon a box hidden in a crevice between two hay bales. It had been pretty at one time, gold with an elaborate painting on top. Through the rust, I can barely make out a boy dressed all page like, with the poufy short pants and tights. He's blowing a really long trumpet in front of a grand palace. The colors are faded. I settle myself on a bale of hay and open the box to discover a stash of letters. There's a picture of a handsome man on a motorcycle right on top. I study the picture closely. Who is this man? As I remove the first letter from its envelope, I quickly realize it's a love letter written to my Mom. Secrets. I quickly put the letter back into its envelope. I hurry to climb down the ladder with the box tucked under my arm. I need to get to my secret spot to explore this new lead. This just might be what I've been looking for. I slide the box into my satchel.

After saddling Ginger up, we begin to work our way through the woods to the back gate. My hideout is on Mr. Stanford's property. I hop down, prop the gate open and lead the crew through. As usual, we're being followed by a couple of dogs. Chi-Chi's riding up with me, of course. The gate secure, I climb back up and we begin our journey. No one can find us now. No one knows about my spot.

Crossing the creek is always fun. Ginger loves to take it in a long running jump. There are no words to describe that feeling. I often close my eyes and imagine what flying must feel like. Suspended for a moment, we land softly on the other side. We meander our way up the hill overlooking the creek. There it is—my haven, a cliff high above the treetops, water running below. At the cliff's edge I can look down upon the wood, the trees and the scurry of life. This is the place where I come to think.

My sacred space, just God and the animals, no people allowed. The sounds of nature, the birds singing. It's a beautiful day, sun shining; with the slight breeze the leaves are making their own song. I climb down and let the reins drop to the ground. Ginger can graze while I play detective. I quickly remove my satchel and slip the box from its hiding place. My belly is tingling with excitement, and my mind is already building stories. Love letters, a stack of them. I need to know more about this mysterious man on the motorcycle. Maybe he's my real dad. This one doesn't think he's my real dad either, he tells me all the time. So maybe now I can find the truth of how I came to be here. I've always felt out of place, like I don't belong here. I don't know who these people are or why they hate me so much. It's as if I have just risen from the depths of a coma and realize there are a whole lot of strangers circling who claim to be my people.

I find a comfortable spot under a grand old tree and once again remove the lid from the box. Gently lifting the letters one at a time, I begin to read. Hours go by as I lose myself in the tale I'm weaving between the lines. Who was this man? Mom loved him. He loved her. He had moved into the city to work, saving, with plans to come and get her as soon as possible. They had plans to marry and then live happily ever after. Instead she's here. His letters are filled with plans for their future. Was I in her belly yet? He sounds like such a kind man. Looking back to the box I see there is one last letter. The handwriting on the outside of the envelope is different, but the same somehow. With trembling hands I lift the envelope and remove the letter. I open it and glance at the signature. It's not from him. It's from his mother with tragic news of Mom's beloved, being killed in an accident. He died early, such a waste, killed on that precious motorcycle. One of his trips back home…was it to see her? How could she have gone from the nice man in the letters…to **him**? *Little girls need their daddies.* I haven't heard anyone mention this mystery man before. Was it a forbidden love? So many questions. Absorbed in thought, I slip the letter back into its envelope. Back in their original order, I carefully return the letters to their hiding place in the box. I take another moment with the picture. Do we look alike? I put the picture back in its proper place of honor on top of the stack, lid back on.

I get up slowly, give Chi-Chi a snuggle, and move to my customary spot at the cliff's edge. I look out with a bird's view over the tree tops while I get settled into a cross-legged position. I think until the words run dry and my mind becomes very still. I have discovered recently that by staring at a single object and clearing my mind of all thought, my body very still, I can slip gently to the other place whenever I want. The sound of the water catches my attention. My eye finds the creek with a doe at its edge. She looks up, sensing my gaze. Our eyes meet.

The Indalo is a prehistoric magical symbol.
The arch represents Rainbow Bridge, the
bridge between heaven and earth.... Rainbow
Bridge is one of the world's largest known
natural bridges, and has been held sacred
by the American Indians for centuries

I find myself sitting on the large rock next to the path. I'm perched on one of the steps, legs dangling. I can see that Tigua's not too far in the distance, heading my way. He's accompanied today by a beautiful paint mare. She has a long flaxen mane and tail. Her body, white with large liver spots. She reminds me of one of the horses an Indian warrior would ride. She carries herself very regally. With a toss of her head and a whinny she tells me to climb aboard. She has sidled up next to the boulder to gather me from my perch. It's as if the stage were set specifically for this purpose. I throw my leg over and get my seat.

"Hang on now. We are going on a little adventure today before we meet the Teacher," Tigua says.

"Where are we going?" I can barely contain my excitement.

"We thought we would show you around a little," he calls back over his shoulder.

The sun is glistening across all the colors of the flowers that lace the meadow. It looks like a rainbow on the ground. Every so often, sprinkled in there, proudly above them all wave the poppies. Grandma's flower. Moving at top speed, the power grows beneath me. My mind becomes clear and sharp as I begin to feel one with the animal. The thoughts and worries of home are left far behind.

We emerge from the meadow at the edge of a thick wood. Slowing things down a bit, we begin to make our way down the trail. I lose myself in all of the sounds, the animals scurrying through the trees. The birds are making music as if just for us. My breath catches at the sight of the light as it filters through the treetops and bounces off of the dew that is resting on the leaves. In this moment, I feel as though it were all constructed just for me. Right here, right now. In this moment, all is right in my world. As the trees become sparser, I begin to hear the sounds of water. A pool, fed by a waterfall, is coming into view. I love the sounds of flowing water. *The water of life,"* I remember the Teacher once saying.

The vegetation around the water's edge is lush and green, layers and layers of green. I can somehow smell the green, along with a hint of sweet. I notice a rainbow a little farther down the river. It seems to be crossing it, like a bridge. It's like nothing I have ever seen. The colors are vibrant, as if they carry weight, moving, but still at the same time. As we mosey down the river's shore, the rainbow has me mesmerized. The questions are piling up in my throat.

"Tigua, that rainbow, what is it? It looks like it has a life of its own."

"The Rainbow Bridge is the bridge to the village of the elders, the sacred bridge of the people. It only appears for those who are called. The Seer has sent it for you."

"The Seer? The rainbow is here for me?"

"He wishes to speak with you."

"He wants to speak with me? Why? And who's the Seer, anyway?"

"The Seer is the great one of the people. He can show you what has been and is to come. He has something that he wants you to see."

The closer we get to the place where the rainbow touches the earth, the more butterflies decide to take flight in my stomach. Tigua lifts his foot to step onto the rainbow bridge and my rational mind screams. *Wait...Rainbows can't be walked on; they're just light.* But with its denseness it has the appearance of being solid, yet see-through at the same time. My worries don't have time to make it to my lips before the mare takes charge, and over the bridge we go. As I look down through the transparent bridge, I can see the water running under the animals feet.

With determination, I let go of my fears and decide to sit back and enjoy the ride. After all, I'm riding across a rainbow with my friends, in the most beautiful land I have ever seen. At the other end of the rainbow, we are met by a real live Indian with all the feathers and leather clothes, just like in the movies. He nods at Tigua. Without a word, he turns to lead us towards what appears to be a small village.

The tepees are arranged in a circle around a central dwelling. Its position seems to be important. As we enter the circle, we are greeted by an elderly man who holds a great deal of reverence among the people. Tigua lowers his head in a bow and greets the man, referring to him as the Great Seer. I am gently lifted from the mare and guided into the tepee. I look back over my shoulder, hoping that Tigua's going to join us. My nerves melt away as the flap is lifted, and the fragrance of burning sage wafts through the air. I see there is a fire ablaze in the center of the space. A few of the elders have already taken their seats. With Tigua at my side, we take our place to the right of the Great Seer, completing the circle. He lifts a large cup and takes a sip, passing it to the man on his left. The cup makes its way around the circle. Now it's my turn. The liquid on my lips is cold and bitter. I try to hide my distaste as I pass the cup back to the Seer. Next, he lifts a large pipe made from an elk antler to his lips. This in turn is passed to his left. I haven't ever smoked anything before. Thoughts of choking on the smoke flit across my mind as I lift the pipe to my lips. Nice, sweet and very smooth. I notice the feeling of my lungs expanding as I inhale the smoke. Only a little coughing. I become lost in the nice tingly feelings that are circulating through my body when the Seer begins to speak. He lays a hand on my shoulder to bring my attention back to the circle. Tuning into his voice, I begin to see scenes from my life playing out before my eyes: hitting, yelling, Dad lurking in my bedroom.

"Why are you showing me this?" I ask. Tears are streaming freely down my face.

"We want you to see that in God's world, you have been given a great gift. You won't have to make the choice of right and wrong like others. The lines are blurred for them. They can't see; they don't know. The differences between dark and light are very clear in your world. With the pain comes great strength and clarity. Be patient and gather the lessons. Your gifts are many."

The picture softens as it settles on my Grandma piddling around the kitchen, me on her heels. The love for her wells up in my chest.

"She was put with you, June, to protect you," he says.

"But he is still hurting me."

"She is protecting what is important. Your body is just for learning. Like the little metal horse in your Monopoly game. The horse doesn't play the game; *you do*. You aren't your body, June. She's protecting the *real you*—what's inside, what makes you get up every morning in spite of your father. Stay close and learn from her. Her teachings and love will guide you to your gifts."

"What gifts?"

"You have many gifts, June. Your powers are many and great. The time will come when you are ready. Be patient and pay attention."

Suddenly, I find myself sitting under the magnificent tree on the customary rock with the Teacher at my side. I've learned that things can change really fast around here, so I just go with it. The smoldering question burns hot inside of me.

"Is he my father, the motorcycle man, I mean? Is he my Dad?"

"My child, that is of no importance."

"But that man down there, he can't be my Dad. How can I have his blood running through my veins? What if his blood makes me mean and ugly, too? Maybe she was pregnant with the motorcycle man's baby and tricked the devil man."

"It doesn't matter," the Teacher says again. "He contributes only to the playing piece they call June. Not to who you are on the inside. The real you has been around a long, long time and has assumed many different playing pieces. You have fought far worse battles than this one. We can't know the light without knowing the dark, little one. That's contrast. In the game, you were given the brightest of lights and the darkest of darks. The Creator wanted no confusion. Pay attention to the scenery and gather your tools. When all are in place, the path out will be clear. Now put the box back where you found it and utter not a word."

My eyes begin to get heavy with his words, my signal that it's time to go back. *No! Not yet.... I have more questions.* But I'm back on the cliff. Looking around I see everything is just the same, as if I have only just blinked. The doe is still standing at the creek's edge. Our eyes still connected. Time seems to stop here with my visits to the other place.

Celtic symbol for mother

Grandma's my angel. She has raised many, many children. After her husband died, she began taking in the unfortunate ones, kids like me. Oh, how I wish I could be one of them. They're lucky. They get to live with Grandma. I get to visit and then have to go back home. Unfortunately, they always seem to come and get me. At the same time, I know that I can't really stay. Who would take care of Sam and Mom? And then there's the customary anxiousness that comes after a second.... I can't forget about Dad. Who would take care of him? Who would put him to bed at night? ...I can still dream about it though.

At Grandma's I can breathe. I am allowed to crawl up into her lap whenever I feel like it. At night she takes me to her bed and curls in beside me. Under the pile of homemade quilts, snuggled in tight, she weaves stories laced with magic, stories about the fairies pollinating the flowers, or how if you listen really closely, you can hear the trees talking.

"The trees have been here so long and have seen and heard so much," she says. She has stories of the elves who live in the poppies. These are some of my happiest moments.

Grandma is no doormat by any stretch of the imagination. She raised two boys and two girls by herself and has conviction in her truths. She has one boy still left at home, John. She's a busy lady with John and me and whatever unwanted kids happen to be around, plus her real job. She's a decorated Stanley dealer, selling women's home products door to door. When she isn't dealing with us, she's making deliveries or having home parties.

Grandma's house is situated right in the center of town on a street they forgot to finish. There's some land back behind her house. Uncle John and some of the boys built a tree house in one of the huge old trees, down the hill a little. No girls allowed. I feel cheated, of course, which stirs my disgust at being put in this delicate little body. *Maybe if I had chosen a different playing piece, they would all just leave me alone.*

There's a chicken coop up the hill a little. My great grandmother and my great aunt live just up the way, and Uncle Clarence, just past that, in an old ramshackle trailer with his family. My great grandmother's house was built from the sides of railroad cars atop an old foundation. Dad and the uncles worked hard building it. We have the whole corner. I love being able to wander around the three places. The only problem is the chicken coop. I have to get through the chickens to get from place to place. It takes every ounce of nerve I can muster to open that gate. I run like it's my last race, with the chickens flapping behind. Grandma provides chicken and eggs. Dad's green thumb contributes the veggies. It's quite a project at harvest time. I have an uncle with a few head of cattle and a few hogs. We all eat well.

Grandma's little house has a side porch and a front porch with swings on every end. It's surrounded by flower beds. All of the seedlings have been dug up on the side of the road somewhere, or have arrived as gifts. Up in one corner is a large bed of poppies.

The police come by periodically to count them. Apparently, she can only have so many poppies. All of her gardens are surrounded by the beautiful stones she has gathered on her adventures. I'm sure we have to be the richest people on earth, with our gardens edged in diamonds. She loves crystals. She wears turquoise on every finger, the protection stone for travelers, she says. She loves to travel in her quest to retrace the steps of the Indians. She always comes back from her trips with fabulous stories. Among the special treasures that find her on the way, she always has a new little figurine for me, a totem carved of stone for my little medicine pouch.

I walk with her through the woods, basket in hand. She knows the names for every plant we pass, which ones are edible, which ones are poisonous. We often come home with greens for our dinner or medicine for an ailment. She knows how to brew up teas out of tree roots or flower combinations.

"God provides for all our needs; we will never go hungry. The earth will always feed us. If you're in doubt, watch the birds. If the birds can eat it, so can you."

Grandma's schooling went through the eighth grade, which she finished in six years. From that point, she worked in the tiff mines to help support her family. Her father and sister had health challenges, so it fell to her to keep the family fed. She worked hard digging in the mines, coming home exhausted, doing it all again the next day.

Grandma has always had a flair for fashion. She can create the most beautiful dresses out of nothing. Grandma loves dresses; she wears a dress almost every day. She sews for me all the time. My great aunt loves to make dolls' clothes. Me and my dolls, we dress pretty well.

Her house is a shrine to God—statues, big and small, on every surface, inside and out—crosses, prints, the Last Supper over the sofa, framed needle-points of Jesus. The Catholic Church is just up the hill. Walking to church with Grandma is a treat. She never gets tired of my questions, and I never run out of questions, especially when it comes to God. The teachings I get from religion class often conflict with the teachings of the Teacher. Grandma, in her soft, self-assured way, weaves the two together in a way that makes sense.

She loves to sing in the name of the Lord, and she does so at the top of her lungs. She doesn't care what others think, and a song bird she is not. I love it. Cooking's right there in the same category. She's definitely not the greatest cook, but she loves to feed people. Usually, guests try to get there early in order to "help." The combinations she thinks to put together should never be tried. Her bread is the exception. I can smell it now as the house fills with its sweetness. Her rolls are her specialty. They're soft, airy, and slightly sweet. On these days, the kitchen's filled to the brim with people waiting for that first pan to be pulled from the oven. Warm, slathered in butter, there's nothing like it. Her light bread buns are the talk of the town, those and her peanut butter cookies. That's pretty much the extent of her repertoire. It doesn't matter what she puts on the table in the end; she loves to feed people, and people love to be there. Everyone leaves feeling like they've been a guest at a feast.

I'm not figured into the family structure with the cousins. In Grandma's eyes, I'm sort of up on the limb with my Mom, as if we were sisters. It's kind of a weird place to be, except when I'm at her house; then it seems perfect. I have respect there, and I always get the first roll from the oven, even if the whole bunch has to wait for me to get there. They just have to wait; that's all there is to it. Her little Junebug gets the first roll. She has it all buttered and waiting for me. No one's allowed to eat until I take the first bite. I always play it up big just to watch her beam, butter dripping down my chin.

When I am in Grandma's house, she is the boss. Dad, for some reason, has the utmost respect for her. A respect that he shows no other, I marvel and revel in that. I seldom leave her side. When the mess of kids is off playing, I'm following her around, asking questions. She never seems to tire of it.

Her house is always filled with music. There's always someone off in a corner or perched on the edge of the porch with a guitar. That's a gift that skipped me, so I settle for watching. I love to witness the strumming as it turns into song.

Tree of family and relatives

Most weekends the group gathers at either Grandma's house or our place. We have the most space for the kids to play outdoors, and Dad's a great cook. Barbecue is his specialty. The grounds are set up with every yard game you can think of: volleyball in the corral, badminton and jarts in the front yard, croquet and horse shoes on the side, Dad's huge hand-crafted stone grill out front. Rain or shine, that's where you'll find him, clad in his black socks, tennis shoes, and umbrella hat—a yellow and red umbrella hat. He's got a cigarette hanging from his mouth, beer in one hand, tongs in the other. He's in his glory. People usually begin to gather after church with their covered dishes and meat, and coolers of soda and beer, kids piling out of the cars. Fun times, until Grandma leaves. Then the party gets underway in earnest. The furniture gets pushed aside and the dancing and poker games start up. As the night wears on, Dad's condition deteriorates. The job of seeing to him is left to me, be it keeping him dressed (he has a habit of undressing when he gets tired), talking him out of a fight, or preventing him from drowning in the toilet or on his own vomit. It's my job. I don't understand Mom's disappearing act. Where is she? Somehow it's as if I am the wife. When did that begin? When he started slipping into my room?

Universal symbol of peace

Grandma's house at the holidays is the place to be. Christmas, Thanksgiving, Halloween, Easter, it doesn't matter. She does them up right. Lots of decorations and lots of play. It's amazing how many people we can squeeze into such a tiny place. We do it, and do it with joy. At Christmas time, Grandma's tree is always a cedar. Dad usually cuts it for her. She likes them as big and fat as will fit in the house. Most of the time, it starts out scraping the ceiling and has to be trimmed down to make room for the angel on top. She decorates it with ornaments that hold the name of every child, even the ones traveling through. They are always treated just like the rest of us. If we have an ornament, so do they. They love seeing their names and the names of all the kids that have ever lived with Grandma, mixed right in with all of ours. It helps them feel they belong somewhere. She'll either rush out to have them made, or if there's not enough time, we'll make them one. There seems to be a lot of kids who show up right before the holidays. All the grownups do it up big for whatever kids happen to be with us. We always make sure they get a real Christmas with lots of presents, some maybe for the first time.

I always try to be there for tree trimming with Grandma. We do it at home, but it's not the same. There's always the stress of what could happen at home. At Grandma's, it's just pure fun, no strings, no expectations. She takes each ornament out one by one, reading each child's name. Then we find the exact, perfect spot. It's a process that can span the length of the evening. We sit and string popcorn for hours listening to her stories. She loves her big colored lights, like the ones we put outside now.

Dad loves Christmas, too. It's usually a pretty good time leading up to the event itself. On tree cutting day, the troops gather, leaving a pot of something warm simmering on the stove. The tree farm is a magical place. They take us out on a big horse-drawn sleigh and leave us to the process of choosing. Families head off in different directions and plan to meet back at our house later for dinner. Sam and I, hand in hand, run from tree to tree in search of the perfect one, the one that wants to go home with us. Once decided, Dad does the duty of chopping it down. A little twinge of sadness wells up in my chest every year at the sight of the tree falling, dying. With a little prayer of thanks, the moment passes. Excitement replaces sadness as the tree hits the ground with a thud. Dad and Kenny pull the tree into the clearing so the sleigh can take us back up to visit with Santa. On the ride in, I fill Sam's head with stories about Santa and the reindeer.

"You'll have to be really, really good for Santa to come. Think for a minute. What is that one special thing? What do you want the most from Santa?"

As we climb from the sleigh in front of the Christmas tree house, we enter Christmas full blown—the smell of pine and cedar in the air; fresh wreaths hang from the walls; sweet, homemade Christmas goodies line the counters. Santa's in his chair of honor, front and center. I take Sam's hand, and we race to be the first of our crew in line. Excitement dances in his eyes as he thinks about his turn on Santa's lap. It makes me happy. I live vicariously through his innocence.

We gather every year at Grandma's on Christmas Eve with lots of singing and lots of food. Always music. The guitars usually get pulled out after a while, and we sing hymns and carols, right up until the moment we have to leave for Midnight Mass. The gifts always end up being the least important part of the evening, even for the kids. Except one, every year Dad sneaks my great Aunt Dee Dee a bottle of Jack Daniels. Grandma doesn't allow alcohol in her house; that's why Dad makes so many trips to the car. It's a well-known secret...just between Dad and Aunt Dee Dee. He makes a to-do every year as if it were the first time. They laugh and whisper, acting as if Grandma doesn't know. Aunt Dee Dee is such a sickly little lady. Dad says, "If a little swig of Jack is going to take away her pain for a second, then let her have it."

At the end of the evening, right before we need to leave, the Bible is pulled out. We finish the night with the story of Jesus' birth, setting the stage for Midnight Mass. Dad doesn't do church, but he does do Midnight Mass. He leaves a few times to get a nicotine fix, accompanied by a swig of his liquid gold, but he's present. We're all in our Christmas wear, dressed to the nines in shoes that hurt our feet, clothes that don't bend right. Hand in hand, I stand next to Grandma and watch her glow turn to rapture as she sings out in the name of the Lord. Poorly, but she doesn't care, and neither do I. Looking up, my heart swells with love. I sure do love my Grandma.

Everything is always tempered with the ever-present dread of going home. After Midnight Mass we hurry home, to our house. Big day tomorrow. I hurry Sam into his jammies with tales of Santa. We hurriedly make up a plate of cookies and pour some milk to set out for Santa. We add a few carrots and celery for the reindeer. *They probably need a snack, too. They've been working really hard pulling that sled around.* Hopefully Dad remembers to take a few bites. I tuck Sam in with me, whispering magical stories about the night until he drifts off to sleep. I don't want his dreams to be affected by the fighting. As I drift off, I plan my reactions for morning so we don't get off on the wrong foot. The trick is to watch Dad's face closely in order to anticipate which gifts he's picked out and what expectations he has. If we don't guess right, the rest of the day will be filled with threats of packing everything up and returning it.

"Spend all that money and these God damn kids don't appreciate anything."

So much for the magic of Santa.

To the Chinese the Yin Yang enclosed in a lotus symbolizes ultimate purity and perfection

When I start my period, a whole new set of obstacles seems to be laid out before me. On that day I'm lying in bed, sure I'm dying. The pain in my stomach is unbearable. It feels as if something is struggling to be set free inside of me. Ripping and tearing, it hurts so much. I can hear them in the other room. Dad's trying to convince Mom to come talk to me. She won't. The fight escalates.

"She needs to know what's happening to her. She thinks she's sick. This is a time when girls need their Mom; she needs to hear it from you."

By this time, I'm sure I'm dying, that I have some rare form of cancer or something. It shouldn't just hurt like this for no reason and with all this commotion. Dad comes in, finally. I guess he decides he's not going to convince her. In a rare moment of compassion, he pulls up a chair. Taking my hand, he explains to me that I am starting my period.

"There's nothing to worry about; everything's normal. You're gonna have some bleeding. The things you'll need are in the bathroom closet when it's time. Have they talked about it at school?"

"Yes, but they never talked about it hurting like this. We had a class on it in the sixth grade, but no one said anything about this part."

He hands me a couple of aspirin and a glass of water. "Now get some rest," he says as he leaves the room.

The next day he gives me a pair of purple vases with little white flowers on the front as a gift.

He has his moments.

It seems with this new development, I have a new scent about me, like a dog in heat. The predators begin appearing at every turn.

When linked with the panther,
one gains the ability to deveolp clairaudience,
the ability to hear communications from
other dimensions or other life forms

The day has come for us to leave our tiny little Catholic school and move on. High School. It will be a big change, moving from our private group of twenty five to the public high. New people, new thoughts. After nine years together we are pretty sick of each other. We are all excited but a little afraid of the newness, too. Leaving the comfort of our tiny little school where everyone knows everyone.

It's the day we have been waiting for all year: graduation day. We are all dressed in our special graduation clothes. The girls, in our fancy dresses, are having a little trouble walking in our brand new high heeled shoes. The boys, with their hair combed just right, in suits and ties, are pulling and tugging at their collars. Complaining. We have all been gathered in our classroom. Everyone is talking at once. Sister Mary Alice takes her spot at the front of the room and quiets us. She begins her speech about how much we have added to the little school and how much we will be missed. I'm not so sure that's right; we were a pretty rowdy bunch. She follows her talk with a prayer. After a moment of silence we are lined up in our customary manner, smallest to tallest. I'm not complaining; I'm always in the front. We walk in a line and file into the pews. Mass begins.

During the service, my mind wanders to the rest of the day. We are all gathering at Grandma's after the service.... I'm suddenly startled from my daydreams by a voice, ringing out through the church, as if it were coming from the heavens. I crane my neck to see where this mesmerizing sound is coming from. He's up in the choir loft, but I can't see his face. My whole body tingles with each note. All I can think of is that voice, big and velvety. I'm swept away, riding the waves as the notes flow out like ribbons of melted chocolate. I spend the entire service waiting for the next song. Then right as Father is holding up the host, I hear a familiar voice, *Pay attention, he's the one.* I look around and see that no one seems to have heard him but me. The Teacher has never spoken to me in this place when others are around.

As this mystery man's music fills the church for the final time, I poke my friend Sally and whisper, "I'm gonna marry him someday." She snickers at me and whispers back, "Yeah right." I say nothing, no need to argue. I know.

I immediately set out to find out what I can about this man without a face. It isn't hard. He's one of the Carney boys. Bob Carney. The Carneys are a large, prominent Catholic family in town. Lots of kids. He has eight brothers and two sisters; the youngest of the boys. They are all well educated, attorneys and business owners. He has nieces and nephews my age. Bob doesn't live here anymore, he's just home for a visit...he moved away to be an actor in New York.

He'll be back.

Our lives are woven by our choices and actions

I am able to keep Ginger on one condition: I have to show her in competition. Dad wants to join the saddle club. Have to show to be in the saddle club. The club consists pretty much of all the people my parents hang out with, along with a few relatives, of course. He found a great old roping cowboy to train Ginger and me together. He teaches me not only to just ride, but to feel and anticipate the animal's next move. He has Ginger stopping on a dime. I learn to guide her with my knees. Great for bareback, I can just run out and jump on, no gear needed.

I really don't enjoy showing one little bit. Dad's always standing at the end of the ring, giving us orders as we pass him. Ginger-side steps every time, and we get thrown out of the ring. She walks wide circles around him. He's not her favorite person, for sure. He'll meet us at the gate mad at us for screwing up the ride.

"What the hell was that?" he says.

"If you would just go stand somewhere else, we would win the whole damn thing," I'd say…not out loud, of course.

Not that I really care. It's the silliest thing under the sun—riding around in circles when we could be out amongst the trees with the wind in our hair. It's the price I pay for the days I get to roam free.

My parents spend every spare moment with two other couples and Uncle Vernon and Aunt Carol. The eight of them do everything together, right down to sharing their partners. They think I don't know, but they think I don't know lots of things. Randy Simons, one of the four men, has started hanging around. It seems everywhere I turn, there's Randy. He'll just happen to be walking past my horse trailer, or he'll be right there at the gate when I'm ejected. It feels good to hear him acknowledge that Dad messed up our turn in the ring. He hops on back to catch a ride over to the cook shack. He tells me how great I look out there. Lots of horse talk, to reel me in. Randy's handsome, with sandy red hair, and twinkly eyes that seem to change color with his mood. Kind of Robert Redford-ish. He has a contagious sparkling smile coupled with all the right words. Quite charming. I've never had anyone pay that much attention to me. I enjoy being caught up as I walk by. Sometimes he gives me a little peck on the cheek.

Then comes the real kiss behind the horse trailer, along with the words of course. My head's spinning. He's kissing me like the grown-ups kiss. I'm sure it's some kind of mistake. I have no idea what to do with the feelings that are moving through my body. A weird excitement, mixed with dread. He wanders away smiling like he has some big secret. I have nowhere to put this new experience, so I decide it's best to go on with life and push the thoughts away. Let's just pretend it didn't happen. It was just a mistake.

Forget it.

The Pempansie is a West African symbol meaning readiness, steadfastness and hardiness

There's always lots to do on show day. I'm up bright and early. With the horses fed and watered, I wander down to the rabbit cages. I have a little time to kill while Ginger's having her breakfast. My favorite of the little furry creatures is Gents. He's solid black with just a few white hairs on his crown, as if he were starting to grey. I lift him from his cage and pull him in close. I give him a good hug. We find a nice spot of clover. I chatter on and on as he has his special breakfast. I tell him about all the things I have to do this morning to get ready for the show. He looks up at me occasionally just to let me know he's listening. After breakfast, he climbs back into my lap for another snuggle. Hugging him tight, I tell him it's time for Ginger to get her bath, and I put him back with the others. I always hate that moment. No one should have to live in a cage, but they do.

Back in the barn, I gather up the supplies—a bucket, a couple of brushes and the hose—and haul it all up to the corral. Ginger still has her head in the hay, so it's pretty easy to sneak up on her. She hates the bath. She doesn't like water much, doesn't like getting her feet wet. Her tendency to walk a mile around a puddle, or jump it, is a problem sometimes in the ring.

She does enjoy the attention, though, so I start talking. "You know you want to be pretty in front of all those people," I croon. The chatter keeps her at ease while I get situated. I begin the process by brushing her from head to toe. Ginger loves being brushed. She nuzzles me with her nose every time I take a break. It makes me laugh, but gets me back to work. I grab the hose and tell her, "Okay, it's time for the water now. It's all right, it's gonna feel good." She looks at me, then the hose, and shakes her head with a snort. She's completely unconvinced. I turn the sprayer on lightly, like rain at first. Ginger whinnies and tosses her head around. After a second or two, she decides it's not so bad after all, feels pretty good in fact. Sudsed up and rinsed off. It's a hot summer day, so she'll enjoy basking in the sun while she dries.

"Now see, that wasn't so bad, was it? You know you feel better. I need to work on the saddle a little bit. I'll be back in a few." I'm off to the barn. I give the saddle the once over and realize it is in need of a good cleaning. That's gonna take some elbow grease. I guess we've played pretty hard since the last show. I grab the saddle soap and get to work. I scrub and buff until it looks as good as new. Satisfied, I haul all of the tack up to the trailer. Ginger's getting bored; she lets out a snort with a toss of her head.

"I'm coming," I tell her. "We still have some primping to do. We have to get these nails polished and that tail, it's a mess. We have to get that mane in shape too. Looks like you got caught up in the brush or something."

All finished. I stand back and admire our work.

"Wow! You look beautiful." Her coat glistens in the bright sunlight. "Okay girl, now it's my turn to get prettied up."

With that, I hurry inside; it's getting late. I make my way back to my room and throw open the door to my closet. I pull out my suit and hold it up to take a look. I like it. It's silly that you have to wear a goofy suit in the first place, but since you do, it might as well be a cool one. Mom made mine. She can sew almost as good as Grandma, when she wants. I got to pick the color. It's purple with pearl white snaps down the front. I also got to pick out my hat. It's pink cotton candy with a purple sash. I tie a pink scarf around my neck. After slipping on my boots and pulling my hair back with a purple ribbon, I step back to take a look in the mirror. For a silly suit, not bad. Time to get going. With a little coaxing, I talk Ginger into the trailer. She knows exactly where we're going—not her favorite place. The cooler's in the back of the truck, of course. Dad and I ride together the few miles to the show grounds. The others will be along shortly.

As we pull in, Randy directs us into a spot between him and my Uncle Vernon. Randy catches me up from behind as I'm getting Ginger settled in. He gently takes my arm and guides me into the trailer. Tucked away and safe from view, he's laughing softly. I'm taken completely off guard. I have pushed the last time far from my realm of thought. I'm not sure what to think or do. I'm frozen. He kisses me again. This time, his hands wander up my back. I begin to feel all tingly but gaggy at the same time. Kissing is kind of gross with all the slobber and the tongue thing. Then his hands find their way to my tiny breast. The guilt wells up in my chest like a fire threatening to burn me up. What about his wife, his girls?

I squirm and wiggle my way free. I rush away to bury myself in the safety of the crowd. I can hear him laughing as I try to become invisible. I can't make sense of it. My mind and body are saying two completely different things. I find a group of girls that I know and put the confusing stuff out of my mind. I'm good at keeping secrets. Randy seems to know that somehow.

It's about time for our turn in the circle. Ginger and I have a good long talk. "Dad's not going to have any effect on us tonight. We're not afraid of him at all. He can't hurt us. There's a fence between us, right? He's on the outside. So we're just gonna pretend like he's not there. We're gonna go right past him without noticing him at all. All right girl? Is it a deal? Let's show him."

There he is at his post, with his customary cigarette hanging from his mouth, beer in his hand. I feel Ginger tense at the sight of him. We make it around that time. She settles back down as we get further away. The next round's good too. It looks like it's gonna be an okay night.

But, there he goes, barking commands, and Ginger sidesteps, startled. Out of the ring we go. Dad's curses are bouncing around. Circles done, I take a deep breath. At least I'll make it out of here before he gets around to the gate.

Randy's waiting and climbs on behind me. He takes the reins and guides us away from the crowd. It's getting dark by this time. He's talking and laughing, the next thing I know we've left the open clearing and are entering the woods. My stomach lurches in a signal of danger. Sliding down easily, he lifts me from my seat. More soft, sweet talk. The kisses start again. His hands begin to roam. This time he unbuttons my jacket with one hand and slips his other hand down my pants.

"Oh see, there, you like it. Look how wet you are," he whispers in my ear.

All of these new feelings...my head is swooning and screaming at the same time. He guides my hand to that bulging place between his legs. Unzipping his jeans he set himself free in all of his glory. He guides my hand in a rhythm that gives him pleasure. I become aware that none of this feels foreign. Somehow, I know just what to do to bring him to that point. The point of those soft noises. I'm just not sure how. He then places his hand on my head, gently pushes me to my knees and prompts me to take his manly part into my mouth. Again, somehow I know what he wants. When satisfied, he steps back, zips his pants and pulls me to my feet.

I concentrate with all my might, fighting the need to gag. I allow him to help me get back on my horse with explanations of it being *our little secret*. We leave from different areas of the woods, so it can stay that way. We don't want to draw any unwanted attention. Not that anyone would care anyway.

How did I know these things? How did I know what to do? It feels like I have done those things before. How was that possible? I've never even had a boyfriend. Never been kissed, outside of Randy. I can't remember.

The encounters become more frequent when I'm forced into babysitting for Randy's two little girls. They are both school age. I don't usually pay much attention to kids. It took some work to get me to agree. "*It's money,*" my parents say as they shove me out the door. Not that I really have a choice, but I finally agree. It's become normal for him to take me back to their bedroom before they leave for their date. Their girls often tell me how much their dad likes me. I wonder if his wife just doesn't care. She seems, from where I stand, to find the situation a little funny. Or is it just easier?

"He talks about you all the time," the girls often say. I wonder if he slips in to their room at night. Car rides home often turn into parking on a gravel road. With time, he has become even more brazen. He seems to love the excitement around getting caught. He's been picking me up at my house. My parents override my protests and force me to go with him. He usually has some sort of excuse about needing my help with something or other. My parents push me out of the door saying, "Now go on. Don't be silly."

Sometimes I find him waiting for me after school. There he is lurking somewhere on the route to Grandma's. After the shows, he climbs onto my horse with me. Last week he guided Ginger right up to where my parents were standing, with his hand down my pants, fingers inside. He knows, I guess, that Dad's gonna be too drunk to notice and Mom pretends not to.

Reminds us to be *aware* of keeping
our *value* of God and the spirits above
the works of man and possessions

U ncle Vernon and I have a special bond through horses. Aunt
Carol is my Mom's only sister, so she and Uncle Vernon
are around all the time. He went to college, in our small
town, that is a big deal. They even lived in California for a while.
They're the only people I know, who have ever lived anyplace else.
He's very calm and soft spoken. I can always count on him if things
are out of hand, the voice of reason. Uncle Vernon never drinks; he
doesn't have a taste for the liquid gold.

He raises Appaloosas. With me being so small, I can get them
used to having a mount early, without any damage being done to
their backs. This gives Uncle Vernon a little head start with the
training. I spend a lot of time at their place working with him.
He has big dreams of having a national winner. He can't get there
without a good rider. I want nothing more than for that rider to
be me, so I jump when he calls. I work hard to prove that I have
what it takes. Spending my days with the horses sounds like a

dream come true. He's my chance to escape this place, to have a life outside of here.

Time for another horse show. The family will be along later, so Uncle Vernon picks up me and Ginger on his way. The ride to the grounds is exciting. Tonight I get to ride Ginger in our usual category, along with one of Uncle Vernon's young fillies in the two-year-old category. I'm talking a mile a minute. We've worked hard this week and are ready. We unload the horses. I walk around with the filly to get her used to the noises. It's her first time out in public with all the sounds and smells. She's nervous, nostrils are flared. I do my best to avoid Randy. He always seems to be hanging around. I have to stay calm and focused, it's important for the filly. It's a big night for us. Can't get my head mucked up. We're saddled up and ready to go. The filly's hyped up. This is a completely different experience from working at home. We walk around outside the ring to get her used to the buzz of activity. I talk to her the whole time.

"Okay girl, it's time to show 'em. You're all right. You can do this." She prances a little bit as we head into the ring. She doesn't like the crowd of horses at the gate, but once we get inside and spread out she settles into a nice rhythm. We get around the ring once. "Yeah, there you go. Great job," I tell her. Horses are picked off periodically, but not us. There we are, first time out. standing in the line at the center of the ring waiting for the announcer to call out the winners. He begins with fourth place. My stomach is in knots as we wait. Now second. Not us either. Here we go…. I can't believe it: First place! That ought to mean something to Uncle Vernon.

I am so excited on the ride home that I can't stop talking. Uncle Vernon just listens. We left my parents at the grounds. They are helping with the clean-up. We unload Ginger and get her settled in for the night. I thank him for the ride and turn to head inside.

Gently he takes hold of my arm and he pulls me back in, close. He kisses me gently on the lips. His hand climbs up my shirt, touching my small little breasts. My brain screams, *No...not you too! This can't be happening! Please don't ruin this, please!*

He's talking softly, telling me, "Don't be afraid. No one has to know. It's our little secret." There's that word again. "You know how special you are to me. This is what people do when they like each other a lot. You like me a lot, don't you?"

My mind is churning; I pull away and sprint towards the safety of the house. They'll be home any minute, I hope. He doesn't follow me. He let me go...this time.

I feel like I'm being hunted.

# Denotes a metaphysical weighing

om and Kerry, one of the four couples, have a pool in their yard. It's a blazing hot day. We are all gathered for a day in the water and a BBQ. I've had the feeling of bugs crawling in my stomach all morning. Everyone is lazing around the pool. Alcohol is flowing freely, except for Mom and Uncle Vernon, they don't drink. All of us kids are in the pool, playing.

Here comes Randy off the diving board with a big splash. We all scatter, giggling. His girls climb up his arm and dive from his shoulders. Before you know it, he has a line of kids waiting for their turn. All fun and games until he decides it's my turn. I've been trying the invisible thing, but I guess it didn't work. He has easy access today, with my bikini. His fingers inside. If I reach out, I can touch Sam. I look over to where my parents are sitting and lock eyes with my Mom. How can she not know what's happening to me? Right here, right here in front of everyone. Thank God, it's finally someone else's turn. He moves right on to the next kid without hesitation and I make my exit. I lift myself from the pool and head into the house to catch my breath. I need a minute to gather myself up, put my face back on. I hear the door of the house open as I make my way back to the bathroom. I take as long as I feel I can get away with, without looking too suspicious before emerging. I find that Aunt Carol has followed me into the house and seems to be waiting for me. She starts with some nonsense small talk then moves gradually into the heavy stuff. I can feel she's nervous and a little upset. Did she see?

"Is he touching you in the wrong way?"

What am I going to say to that? *Yes…almost everyone out there is touching me in the wrong way, including Uncle Vernon.* If I tell her, God only knows what will happen. What if they blame me? They already know. They have to. I could see the whites of Mom's eyes just now. If it's all brought out in the open like this, in front of people, Dad will kill them.

Keeping Dad out of prison feels important, I'm not sure why. I don't want anyone to get hurt; I just want to be left alone. I don't want anyone to die.

Or…what if they don't care at all?

I decide not to risk it, and lie.

Panther is connected with sexual energy,
we are taught to embrace these energies
as true power and direct them
consciously without judgment

I close myself in the darkness of my room with the questions churning, thoughts colliding. I think and pray, and pray and think, until my head is empty. In the stillness I drift off to the other side easily. I am met tonight by a beautiful Indian woman. She seems to be in her mid–twenties, kind brown eyes.

Looking at me directly, she says, "June we have some important things to talk about today. It's okay for us to talk freely here. You can say whatever you need to say and I will try to help you understand."

She urges me with a gesture of her hand to walk beside her.

"Where's Tigua? He always meets me here," I'm not budging without Tigua.

"No worries, little one. Tigua is waiting for us in the village."

"Are we going to meet with the Seer?"

"Later. We have some things of our own to do first."

Intrigued, I decide to follow. "Are you sure Tigua is there?"

"Shh," the woman hushes me while touching my hair. "Nothing is going to happen to you here. You are safe."

Up ahead, galloping to meet us is the most beautiful white stallion I have ever seen. He tosses his head and whinnies his greeting to us both. Bringing up the rear is my new friend, the Paint. After our hellos, we are offered some company and a lift. Situated and comfortable, we begin our journey to the Seer's village.

"Do you live in the village, too?" I ask.

"Yes. The Seer is my father."

A pit is forming in my stomach. *Does he hurt her too; is that what they all do? He felt like such a good man. Is there such a thing? Every time I put my trust in one, the ugly, confusing stuff starts.*

As if reading my thoughts, the woman says, "That's what we are here to talk about today, June. All men aren't bad. Some people do bad things, make bad choices, that affect you, but they all come from God in the beginning. They all start with the same pure essence. If you look closely, you can see how frightened and insecure they really are. On the inside, they feel like angry little children. Growth has stopped for them."

The rainbow appears up ahead. The ride over the bridge never ceases to amaze me. The colors are dancing and gyrating, transparent yet solid. I look back and watch as the bridge disappears from sight. Arriving at the village, we stop in front of the entrance of a small tepee on the edge of camp. It is situated some distance from the others. There's nice warm smoke coming out of the opening at the top. The feeling of comfort is right on the heels of the familiar smell of sage and lavender. I'm helped from the Paint's back by a very handsome young man. I try not to notice the gentleness of his touch, the sweetness in his face. I turn away quickly. Uncle Vernon's betrayal is more than I think I can bear. I have given up hope of any man being true and kind. I've never known one. The Seer and Tigua are waiting for me outside the entrance.

"June, you have a big job ahead of you. It's up to you to untie the karmic knots of your lineage. It's time to find your courage and see what is before you."

With a wave of his hand, I am shown a beautiful pool of calm water. One by one, women come bursting through the surface of the water as if they've been held under too long. By the time the show's over, more women than I can count have risen from the water, leaving as many men lined on the shore. With this, the flap is lifted and the Indian woman and I, along with Tigua, are left alone inside.

The woman guides me to a lovely spot, all cozied up with blankets and pillows of all colors. She urges me to get comfortable and relax. It won't take much with all of the colors and the aroma.

I realize that I haven't even asked the woman her name, "I don't know your name."

The woman sits close. She pulls the pipe from its place and takes a long pull. As she passes it to me she says, "My name is Mahala." I can feel the familiar sensation working its way through my body after my turn with the smoke.

"What does it mean?" I close my eyes for a moment. I want to take it all in.

"It means the power of the female," she says. She takes another pull from the pipe and places it back in its rightful place. "Now, I understand that there are things going on down there right now that are very confusing for you."

I nod my head yes. "Why does this keep happening? I don't understand. We were taught in kindergarten to keep our hands to ourselves. I don't want them to touch me. Anyway, I look like a little boy. It's not like I have big boobs like other girls. Why me?"

"They are like moths at a light, June; you burn brightly, someday for all to see. It's not about what your body looks like or what you wear. You haven't done anything wrong. This is about how you make them feel. They enjoy basking in your glow. It's the only way they know to get close to you. Draining you of your light. It's time for you to see what's been happening with your father. The picture has been moved out a little, June, so you can see. Why do you think things with those men feel so familiar? You have to see. Once you see, then you can stop him. In stopping your father, you stop the others. This is why he hits you June, out of disgust for himself and what he does to you."

But my mind moves on to what is more pressing. "My body betrays me." I don't want to see the woman's face as I speak, but sensing no judgment, I continue. "My mind screams at me with disgust and shame but my body gets all tingly. It makes no sense."

The woman smoothes my hair, soothingly, "June, that's perfectly normal for your body to react to touch. God made us that way. They aren't supposed to touch you like that. It's not their right. It will be their burden to bear, in the end. I want to give you another tool for your medicine pouch. With this you will have a way to diffuse the energy in your body so you can have clarity in your mind."

The woman urges me to lie back. Pouring warm oil in my hand, she guides me to that soft spot between my legs, the place everyone seems so interested in. She gets up quietly, leaving me to explore.

Lifting the flap of the teepee, she turns back to me. "Now relax, June, and find it. Then you will understand their need, and what it is they want from you. It's sacred, and it's yours, June, no one else's. Only to be shared at your will. It cannot be taken."

I am experiencing feelings I couldn't have dreamt of. Colors are swirling in my mind's eye. After the explosion of white light, breathing hard, I lie back and bask in the glow of the moment. I gather myself up, feeling more than a little embarrassed. I have no idea how much time has passed. I slowly work up my nerve to face the village and poke my head through the flap of the tent. I look around and realize life is going on normally. Everyone is going about their business. No one seems to care in the least what I was doing amongst the pile of colorful pillows. They don't know that I have been on a treasure hunt. This makes me smile as I step out. Somehow, I feel a little taller.

"June." I hear Mahala's soft voice call out as she approaches. She puts her arm around my shoulder as she begins to speak. "Now, June, take back with you what you know and take charge of YOU."

With that, I'm back in my bed, body tingling, hand between my legs. Holding that special place tightly, the place that has been touched by everyone but me. Now I understand it is mine; these feelings are mine. I don't want to share a sacred feeling like that with *any* of them.

Chinese symbol for younger brother

Sam's sick all of the time these days. He's so skinny and little. He can't even get on the school bus without help. I have to lift him up to the first step. His ulcers keep getting worse. I start to share with him stories of my adventures in the other place. I tell him all about Tigua, how afraid I was the first time I saw him, how Grandma's there sometimes, but she looks different. I try to weave the teachings of the Teacher through my tales, as much as I can. Right in the middle of a grand story, an idea begins to form. What if I could bring him with me? What if the memory thing would work for him too? Maybe some fun on the other side would be good medicine for him. His poor little body could use a break. I don't remember everything; maybe he won't either. I'm gonna try to take his hand and bring him with me the next time things get tough. We'll see what happens. The excitement grows at the possibilities as I share my idea with him. He tries hard to understand and nods his little head yes, eyes shining. We make plans for a signal.

"You will have to pay attention and listen real close. I'm going to yell your name with my mind. You won't hear me like normal," I tell him. "It'll be like you hear me inside your head, or in your belly. If you feel something at all, hold up your hand. Now, don't take time to think about it, or we might miss our chance."

I'm banking on the idea that maybe we can talk without words, with our minds, like Grandma and I can. Together, we decide that it sounds like a pretty fun experiment. If it works, I can get Sam out of here for a second. The talking with no words thing could really come in handy, if we can master it. It sure couldn't hurt anyway. No one will know what we're saying, unless we want them to. Sam thinks that sounds pretty cool. All said and done, plan in place, Sam looks up and says, "Wherever you go June, I want to go, too."

"Forever and always...forever and always."

I have a promise to keep.

# Denotes a metaphysical weighing

One bright summer day, the whole group is going to Six Flags. Uncle John's summer job has set us up with huge discounts. It's something we wouldn't be able to do otherwise. I'm sticking close to Dad. At this point it's preferable to getting stuck in a group with any of the other men. Not to mention when Dad gets out in public, we never know what might happen.

Hopping from one ride to the next we make our way around to Tom's Twister, the ride that's shaped like a huge barrel. It spins so fast that the centrifugal force pins everyone to the wall as the floor drops out. I tend to get sick from the spinning, but at the last minute, I decide to join them. I'm positioned directly across from my father. Good spot. Dad's situated between a very large lady and Uncle Vernon. The thing begins to spin, slowly at first, then faster and faster, until we are all plastered to the wall, unable to move. I'm keeping my eye on Dad, just in case. I notice fear creep into the large woman's face as the color's draining out. Just at that moment, the floor drops, and the woman lets go of a scream…and her bladder. Large woman, large bladder. The centrifugal force has the pee suspended in midair for a second and then throws it up against the wall…right where my

Dad is pinned. Once again drenched in urine, but this time God has it in slow motion. He can't even move his arms to wipe his face.

As the ride begins to slow and the floor rises, we gain more control over our movements. Dad's wiping at his face with his shirt sleeve, one of the only dry spots he can find, cursing the whole time. The poor lady is so embarrassed. She's talking ninety miles an hour. I make a beeline for the exit. I have to find a safe spot out of sight to relieve my laughter. I sometimes wonder if God throws these little tidbits in the game just to keep me paying attention, or if he just enjoys my laughter. Whatever the reason, it keeps the game interesting. Too bad Grandma missed this one; she would have gotten a kick out of it.

Maiden, mother, wise woman

With two girls of my own, another one of God's little tricks, life becomes consumed with the job of keeping them safe. My search for truth is put on the back burner. No one is left out of the circle of suspicion. I am vigilant about imparting to the girls the lessons I learned too late. No secrets for them. They are left alone with no one until they can speak. My girls have been given the vocabulary to vocalize their discomfort if need be. I don't have to wait long. My youngest is three.

It looks like it's going to be a beautiful Easter weekend. The family is all dolled up for the Easter Vigil. It's a late night service, ten p.m., on Holy Saturday. Sara, my youngest, is already a little cranky and doesn't want to go in. She's a live wire and has trouble sitting still on a good day. She's begging me to go to the child care. It's housed in the Activities Building, right next to the church. I'm not thrilled about it but finally give in. It's church. It's all good. Nicole, our oldest, decides to join us for the service. The three of us find our customary spot, front row on the left. Nicole wants to be able to see Father.

Toward the end of the service a weird feeling starts in the pit of my stomach. I can't get to Sara fast enough. Wiggling my way through the crowd, I'm finally standing in the doorway of the childcare.

Sara, turning, cries, "Momma."

I scoop her into my arms and tell myself, *"See, she's just fine."* I can't wait to get out into the fresh air. I say my "Thank yous" and we rush back outside. I find a place free from the crowd. I need a view of the doorway to the building so we can catch Bob and Nicole before they go inside. I begin with my usual stream of questions about Sara's evening. "Did you have fun tonight, sweet girl?"

She shakes her head dramatically. "That man," she says while pointing at a man who appears to be helping in the room. "He was itching his pee pee while I was sitting on his lap, Momma."

"What do you mean itching his pee pee?"

"He was itching it up and down."

"Was it inside his pants or did he have it on the outside?"

"He had it on the outside, Mommy. I didn't like it. He wanted to take me to the bathroom. I wouldn't go, but I had to go real bad."

"Did he touch your pee pee?"

She shakes her head no. Catching sight of Bob I wave him over. He can sense something is wrong.

"Sara, can you tell Daddy about the man?"

She reiterates the story verbatim.

"Daddy needs you to show us which man, Sara. Can you do that?" Bob says.

She nods her head eagerly.

We move to the doorway of the room, and she points confidently at a scraggly looking man on the fringe. "Him. He smells funny, Mommy."

The man, startled, takes off.

"Take the girls on home. I'll get a ride," Bob goes after him.

I settle the girls into bed with chatter about the Easter Bunny coming in the morning. I'm perched on the edge of Sara's bed when she asks, "Where's Daddy?"

"It's okay, don't you worry. Daddy went to catch the smelly man so that he can't itch his pee pee in front of any other little girls. He will be home in a little while. Now you just get some sleep. You want to wake up early and see what the Easter Bunny has left for you guys. Right?"

She nods eagerly, and I give her a kiss on the cheek. The phone's ringing, so I close the door on my way out and make my way through the house to the kitchen.

"June, we got him. I was chasing him through town and met a cop stopped at a stop sign. The cop believed me. He caught him about four blocks from the church. Can you believe it? They want Sara to come down to the police station and tell them the story. What do you think?"

"Wow, that's amazing. I think she needs to do this. Don't you?'

"I do."

"Okay, I'll talk to her. We'll be there in a few."

I went back to the edge of Sara's bed. "Sara, that was Daddy. He was so brave. He helped the police catch the bad man. The police need you to tell them everything that you can remember. Can you remember what he looks like?"

"Yes, Mommy."

"Do you think you can do that for Mom?"

She nods her head yes.

Sitting across from a very nice police woman, Sara in my lap, Teddy bear wrapped in her arms, she again tells the story, exactly the same way. She describes the man down to the mis-matched buttons on his jacket, and again with the smell.

When she finishes, the woman smiles. First looking at Sara she says, "You are a very brave little girl. You did a great job. Thank you so much for sharing your story with us."

She turns to us. "That was amazing. She has quite an eye for details. There's not a doubt that we have the right man back there."

"That's my girl. I'm so proud of you," I snuggle her in tight.

The guy got off thanks to some technicality. But for Sara, it was over. She has no leftover scars from that day. She had the vocabulary to verbalize her experience and the safety of knowing that we thought it was wrong. She saw us fight for her.

No Secrets!

To Native Americans,
horse combines the grounded power of the earth
with the whispers from the spirit realm....
He is honored as messenger and helper
of spirit knowledge to the people

Sometimes, we go on these fabulous trail rides, one of the perks of the saddle club. An older guy in the group has a piece of property way out in the country. It's a beautiful spot, rolling hills and lots of trees. There's a stream that flows not far from where we usually set up camp. With horses in tow and loads of food and drink, Dad tries to get there early to stake out the perfect spot for our weekend. Always in control. I like to be close to the water, so I ride with him, maybe throw my two cents in. The tents are set up around a large stone grill. The grate on top is big enough to hold meat for fifty people. I love it. Dad rarely leaves the house without his chain saw, so he and I gather wood from the downed trees for the cook fire. It takes a long time for a fire of that size to burn down enough to cook over. I might be able to get a quick ride in by myself before the crowd shows up, if I'm lucky.

There are usually ten to fifteen families. As people begin to gather, the women busy themselves with the task of keeping us fed. It seems like that's what they do the whole time we're here. No wonder Mom hates camping, horses or no horses. I don't want to get roped into that, so I stay on my horse the entire time, out of sight, if I can manage it. I take the lead on every ride that goes out. All I have to worry about is staying mixed in the crowd. I don't want to get split off and end up out there with Randy or Uncle Vernon.

My favorites are the moonlight rides. Ginger and I have a blast. When we are riding we don't have to think. We can push it all away and make believe that all of life is just like this. Peaceful.

Back at the camp site, plenty of beers already down the hatch, the men end up gathering around Ginger. Uncle Vernon insists I need a better horse. I don't want another horse. She's my best friend, and she's perfect. Uncle Vernon thinks he might get on and show her a thing or two. His butt no sooner hits the saddle; oops...he's in a heap on the ground. My hand flies to my mouth to quiet the giggles that threaten to spring out. He looks around, a little embarrassed, gets right back on.

She dumps him again. It happens so fast. Dad starts chuckling; now it's his turn. He thinks he's gonna show her what's up. He climbs up and settles himself in the saddle. She lets him. He gives her a nudge in the side to move forward. Nothing. She looks over at me with a look that says, *Really?* She has her feet dug in, not going anywhere. A good swift kick. Nothing. He slaps her with the reins. She's glued to her spot, begging me to get him off.

I hurry over. "Dad, she's just tired," I say. "I think Mom's calling you."

A few others, seeing Dad's blood pressure rising, chime in, "Hey, let's go get another beer."

At this point, everyone's working together to diffuse the situation, we all know from experience what this potentially could turn into. One of Dad's temper tantrums would ruin the whole weekend for everybody.

Dad dismounts. "Stupid God damn horse. Just gonna have to get rid of her." Glancing back at her, "She's not worth a damn dime, though."

I stroke her face and plant a huge kiss on her muzzle as we walk away quietly, smiling on the inside.

"I guess you showed them."

Family tree and relatives

There was this little store out in the middle of nowhere. It looked like an old "Beverly Hillbillies" type cabin with a long porch across the front. It had a couple of rocking chairs. There were often a couple of old men out there smoking their cigarettes or chomping their ever present chew. There they sat with their spitting cups in hand, rocking and chatting it up. It was a funny little place. It felt as if you were walking back in time. As you crossed the threshold, there was a potbellied stove to one side with a couple of chairs around it. On the other was a long counter with a glass case below filled with sundry small items from knives to belt buckles. Shelves of dry goods were along the walls. Off to the right was a room that housed jeans and other basic clothes items, like farmer work clothes. The old man and his wife lived in the back.

The trip there was always an adventure. It was not at all like going to a regular store. There were big barrels of shoes, the ones that looked like Keds but not. The trick was finding two the same size, the same color…and then there's the right and left. It was quite a job.

Just a huge barrel of mismatched shoes. Mom and I would summon our patience and one by one pick through them. With some luck, I'd find two in my size that went together. Dad would have the boys back in the room stacked with Wrangler jeans.

Now these jeans were something else. They could stand up all by themselves. I didn't like them. The legs didn't bend right. The jeans had more control over your legs than you did. I would stand in the doorway and laugh on the inside. This was one instance when I was glad to be a girl. At least I could get by with wearing dresses. The boys didn't have a choice. They walked around like robots for a while until they got broken in, usually about the time they started to get too short, or in Sam's case, had big holes in the knees.

Possibility of opening and or closing, possibily secrets

None of the girls on my Grandma's limb of the tree escaped the preying eyes and hands of men—men lurking, waiting until they knew no one was paying attention. Maybell, the youngest of us three, was kidnapped by this Charles Manson-looking guy. Her father, Uncle Clarence, had a good heart but no boundaries. He always saw the good in people, unfortunately the bad slipped by him. So, this guy moved in across the street and gave her dad some sob story about tough times, and suddenly he was an official member of the family, Maybell among his newfound privileges. Still in junior high, she was flattered by this new stranger's attention, his nice words…always with the nice words. You learn not to trust them very much after a while…the words. It wasn't long before he sneaks her out in the middle of the night; no one ever locks their doors around here. By the time anyone realized she was missing, he had her across the state line.

It didn't take long to figure out who she was with. Uncle Clarence waited by the phone for that call. Maybell finally found a way to escape and call home. Looking around she found an address. After a big police bust, they got her home. The man went to jail for a second and came directly after her as soon as he was released, waltzing right into Sunday morning Mass. The men burst out of the church after him, followed by a crowd of onlookers. *Outsiders don't take our things. I guess we're reserved for family.*

To the American Indians,
the black panther was endowed with great
magic and power, a symbol of mastery over
all dimensions.... Indian shamans performed
rituals to shape shift into panther power

An explosion went off this afternoon. I'm sure I've done
something, I'm just not sure what. It escalates very
quickly. I'm being held down on the floor by my father,
his hand is around my throat. I'm watching from above. His hand
is the size of my whole head, his fingers almost meet. My little
neck looks so small in his grip. I can't scream. No air will come
out, not that it would do any good anyway. It doesn't matter. At
this point I've had enough; I decide Sam has too. It's time to try.
I hope it works.

"Enough! Sam let's go!" I call out with my mind.

I see that Sam hears me by the acknowledgment in his eyes. He
concentrates really hard, rises up and takes my hand. I look back for a
moment, watching my body begin to weaken. We come down softly
in the meadow. A squeal of excitement erupts from Sam. Bouncing
up and down, he takes in our surroundings. The joy in his eyes makes
me laugh. It worked! I got him here! I see Tigua in the distance, a
magnificent tiger at his side.

I explain to little Sam, "The animals can all talk here, and there are no mean ones. Don't be afraid."

His wariness of the two approaching cats is more than obvious. I take his hand in mine to help ease his nerves. I can't contain my excitement, so I hurry, dragging him along behind, in order to bridge the distance faster. I throw my arms around Tigua's neck in a warm greeting.

"I'm really glad to see you today, Tigua. Things aren't going so well down there. I'm not sure I'm going to make it through this one."

He greets my hug with a nuzzle and warm happy purring, "I know; I was watching."

"You can see down there?" I ask in amazement.

"Of course. I'm always watching," Tigua replies.

"This is my brother, Sam. Who's your friend?"

"June and Sam, meet Zuni. He's a very dear friend of mine. He's going to have some fun with us today. I want you guys to climb up and settle yourselves in for an amazing ride. A ride like you have never experienced before. Sam, you can ride with Zuni today; June you're with me."

"Are you sure, Tigua?"

"Yes, I want you to feel it, "he replies. "I want you to feel it, June—feel what it feels like to be me, to be a panther. You have panther blood in your veins, you know."

"Panther blood?"

"Shh…June, just feel it. Today is going to be all about fun. It's a surprise. All set?"

We begin to meander down the trail a ways, nice and easy. Then the cats begin to pick up speed. This feeling is like no other, even different from what I feel with the horses somehow. Tigua flies off the trail, making his own way through the meadow. Zuni and Sam aren't far behind. I look back over my shoulder to check on Sam. The smile across his face says it all. He's having the time of his life.

Leaning in close to Tigua, I begin to focus. "Feel it, June. It's time for us to join, to become one," he says, in my head though, not out loud. The energy emanating from his body is electric. Letting go of all thought, I find myself anticipating his every move. Suddenly, we morph into one. I am the panther. I am seeing through his eyes. I see so clearly: every blade of grass, every stream of light, every hair is an antenna…I feel what it is to be alive. I feel the strength of my muscles as they stretch out for the next stride. Amazing the power, the agility. Panther power.

As we begin to slow the pace down, I find myself back on top. The sight before us takes our breath away. Zuni and Tigua slow to a stop and line up side by side. They are giving us a moment to take it all in. Sam and I are speechless. Before us is a playground to top all playgrounds with slides made of rainbows, lollipop flowers, marshmallow clouds, and right in the middle is a castle, a castle that looks as if it were made from spun sugar. After a moment we are back on the move covering the remaining distance. We slide off our rides and walk into a fairytale, where we are prince and princess, and the world is our playground. Sam drags me straight to the castle.

Touching it he giggles, "Can we eat it?"

"I guess so."

He picks off a piece and touches it to his tongue. "It's sugar." He picks a bright red lollipop, and he's off to touch the rainbow. He laughs, darting from one thing to the other. He can't decide what to do first. I love to see him laughing and playing like a normal kid.

Playing. I have never really understood playing, but it's sure fun to watch Sam. At the end of the day, we're laid out in a heap with the cats. We're content and exhausted. Our bellies are full of as many sweets as we can hold. Sam's curled up in my arms; I'm curled up in Tigua's. Zuni is all stretched out basking in the sun. It feels good to see Sam peaceful, free from worry.

As he looks up at me, I witness the cloud come over his eyes, "Can we just stay here, June? Please? I like it here; I don't want to go back." The tears reach the brim and threaten to spill over. "My stomach doesn't hurt here. Please?"

I'm relieved to see the Teacher approaching. I don't know what to say. I try diverting Sam's attention to the visitor. "Look, here comes the Teacher." I'm trying to keep my face on; I don't want Sam to see me get sad. Inside, I want to cry for him, for all of us. They won't let us stay here. I've tried.

The Teacher senses Sam's heaviness and takes him onto his lap. He brings me in close at his side. Looking from Sam then to me, he begins to speak. "You two have to work together now. You have a special gift that is going to be very important to you both from this point on. You don't have to use words anymore to speak. You can use your thoughts. Speak loudly and clearly with your mind, the same as you do with your Grandma, June. This will be a very valuable tool for the two of you in the future." He looks at me intently now. "Remember, June, you and Tigua shifted, became one, today."

I nod my head with excitement.

"You have the energy of the panther running through your veins. Use it. When the time is right, use it, remember. This is an important tool for your medicine pouch, June. Remember."

111

With that, I find myself back at home on the floor gasping for breath. Out of the corner of my eye, I can see Sam's back, too. Dad's fingers loosen on my throat. He shakes his head, stands up, and walks away. I can't cry. I'm just thankful to be breathing, I guess.

There are worse things than dying...being born.

Maiden, mother, wise woman

And then there were the doctors—MD's, Psychiatrists, specialists, psychologists, counselors…clergymen. I ran the gamut, always searching. Searching for a way out. Out of the prison that is my life. I have to keep running. If I slow down, it's going to catch me. The dark, dank slumber—it's always threatening to envelop me. Labels. Their secrets run through me like a virus. A deadly virus. The pain in my body is unbearable, debilitating. Each secret has its own set of symptoms threatening to take me over. One drug leads to the next, the side effects often worse than where I started. Another drug, then another, then another, until I'm taking eleven prescription medications. It's hard to think in here under this drug cloud. The slumber is upon me. All I want to do is sleep. They tell Bob that I'm never going to get better; it's just too much. The doctors quit talking to me. But, inside something is always pushing, pushing me to find the key.

I have been seeing Dr. Randolph for a couple of years now. The first thing he does is slowly pull me off all of the medications. This in and of itself is great progress. At least I can think out in the light, out from under that big gray cloud.

One day he asks, "Why are you here, June? You can spout off everything I could ever tell you."

"I want out. I want to be able to feel. I want to feel normal. Am I crazy? Should I just give up?"

"June, you are one of the sanest people I know. It's not you; it's them. You are not crazy."

"But what do I do with it all? How can I get it out of me, out of my body?"

"Here's what I see. You have all the right facial expressions, all the right responses. You have been a very observant pupil, but you're not in there. Your body is like a puppet."

"Their secrets are taking up so much space; I feel like there's no room for me in here. They're so heavy, I don't want them anymore. I want it all out! I want to be here. I want to feel something other than pain."

"I don't know how to help you, June. I'm sorry. I don't know what to say."

I never went back. No one knows how to help me. I have to find my own way. *"The people you need will come to you,"* I remember the Teacher saying. At this point, having exhausted all traditional means of treatment, I begin reading. I find myself in the bookstore amongst the stacks of beloved books; my arms full. As if waiting, on the floor in front of me is a book on meditation. I have heard the word before but know nothing about it. I decide the book is intended to come home with me. This means I will have to stop running, sit still. It is said to heal the mind and body. After working with the process on my own for a while, I'm led to a teacher. His philosophy coincides with that of the Teacher of long ago. After a while, I pose the question, *How is meditation so different from what came so naturally when I was a girl, how I used to get to the other place? I just did it with my eyes open. It had the same result, the same process, to focus on a single object or thought.*

Back to the beginning.

Guardian angel

You know the saying; "There is always someone worse off than you?" I got to witness that regularly. The number of foster children who came through Grandma's house was astounding. Never was there a time when I thought myself the only one. The kids were always met with a hot meal and a bath. I met a brother and sister who had spent their lives, in an attic with their legs chained to a post. They had never even seen silverware before. I will never forget the looks on their faces as they were trying to figure out what to do with it all. The memory will be glued in my mind forever. People need a license to have a dog. These were human beings! After a few seconds, they just dove in face first.

One poor little boy had been locked up in a closet. He hadn't had a bath in a very long time, if ever. The bath came first this time. His poor skin came off with the grime.

Those were the ones the world could see.

The others look just like me. You wouldn't pick them out of a group and label them as troubled, maybe just a little different. They aren't dirty; they have polite manners. They look just like any other kid, until you look into their eyes. Eyes that have seen and know too much. We go home to lives like a movie where the words and actions are out of sync. People don't know what happens when we go home with these people who are supposed to love us the most. People don't know the secrets that are kept.

It makes me happy that these kids got away and found themselves in my angel's house. Hopefully their war is over.

But I have to go home.

Junebug brings a higher intuitive connection and a keen sense of discernment

My body begins showing signs of all that is going on at home. I am at the doctor's constantly. We exhaust the home town doctor with too many unexplainable visits, now Mom or Grandma drives me into the city. The rides with Grandma are an adventure themselves. She has one speed, fast, and one pedal, GO! I'm not sure how many times I hit the floorboard with her sudden stops and starts. It goes on for years, problems with my stomach, upper GIs, lower GIs. They're never really able to find anything specific. I have developed a rare sort of panic attack; I cough, twenty four seven. I cough until I lose consciousness.

After several visits with Dr. Martin, Mom comes with me. We're back in the doctor's office after a battery of tests to discuss the results, which of course show nothing specific. He looks at me, thinking. He then looks at my mother, pauses, and asks her to leave the room.

Stunned, her breath catches. She gets up slowly and glances back at me. Her look saying more than words ever could. Once alone, he sits beside me taking the chair that had been my mother's. I feel as though he can see right through me.

"June, are there things going on at home, maybe with your Dad, that I should know about?"

I concentrate real hard, trying to see how many dots I can count on the tiled floor as he speaks. Counting helps me stay calm. My mind works at the same time to quickly calculate the risks of answering the man's questions. Maybe he would let me go live with Grandma all the time. But what about Sam? What if he sends me home anyway? I'm sure she's out there making up a story as we speak. If Dad finds out, he'll kill me for sure. Last time was a close one. Then what would happen to Sam?

The kind doctor gently takes my chin in his hand to get my attention, "June, if something's not right, you can tell me. I want to help you."

Inside I'm screaming *YES! YES horrible things happen there*, but just as quickly comes, *but what if I have to go home with her?* She's right out there.

"No," I say, "everything is fine."

"June, you can tell me."

"Everything is fine," I say again. With that, I stand, and he lets me go.

Mom doesn't ask me about those few moments alone with the kind doctor. I guess she knows that if I walked out, I hadn't talked. Secrets.

Panther helps us confront and transcend
those things from childhood which created
suffering and have caused a loss of
innate power and creativity

I keep having this disturbing dream. I have it almost every night. I stumble out of my bedroom in the morning. Rubbing my eyes, I enter the dining room to find the house eerily quiet. I look out the window to see the drive is empty. I spot a note on the kitchen table. I grab it up and read.

"June, we have moved. Didn't want to wake you. Just give us a call when you get up, and we will come and get you," there's a phone number at the bottom of the page.

Weird, I didn't even know we were thinking about moving. With the note still in my hand, I snag a Pop Tart from the cabinet. *I guess I'll give the number a call.* Out of nowhere, there's this odd little guy sitting on a stool in front of the phone hanging from the wall in the kitchen. He looks like a coffee bean, with really long skinny arms. At the end of each arm are these huge white gloved hands, like the Hamburger Helper guy. Every time I have the dream, I try a different tactic to get past him, but no matter how hard I fight, I can't get to the phone. The funny little guy just scoops me back with those huge hands, laughing. He's not scary. He doesn't want to hurt me. He just isn't going to let me get to the phone.

I sneak off to the barn early one morning after a sleepless night filled with this persistent dream. I scurry up the ladder to the loft and find a nice spot among the hay bales to think about my dream. Maybe it's a message and I just can't understand. I always feel so disconcerted the morning after, as if someone's trying to tell me something. Lost in thought, I'm startled by a strong, deep purr behind me. At the highest point in the loft, I see Tigua, all stretched out, relaxing. I'm not sure how long he's been there, but he's looking pretty comfortable.

"Good morning, June. It seems that you're having some trouble deciphering the message from The Seer."

I reiterate the dream for him; my anxiousness builds as I get to the struggle of getting to the phone. I climb up beside him and absent-mindedly run my fingers through his fur. He has a calming effect on me.

"I guess they left a note," I say, pretending to smile.

"There, there, June. You need to see. No matter how hard you work or how hard you struggle, you will never reach them."

"It feels like there's a thick glass wall. I can see them; they can see me, but I can't touch them."

"You are operating from different planes—you awake, they in the slumber. It's like going into a store where the guy at the counter is speaking Russian. No matter how loud you talk, no matter how many times you say what you want, he isn't going to understand. You don't speak the same language, June. When you are in the slumber, your focus is on what things look like, not what they are. They live in an illusion."

"But they are my family."

"Family is a group of people working towards a common goal, June, with love, working towards the highest good for all. It's not the blood running through your veins, or the roof you share. You will someday make your own family, a real family, one filled with love and respect. We all have choices to make; that's the Creator's free will, June. These are their choices. All you have control over are your words and your actions. From a place of integrity, your life and your family will be made. It's time to begin the process of letting go now. Let go of the picture of what you wish. It's just an idea. It's time now to look closely at what is."

The Egyptians shape-shifted through a ritual called *passage through the skin* to bring forth the panther power

Thanksgiving's always my favorite, not as many expectations. It's just a day for everyone to be together and eat lots of good food. Dad and I always go into Grandma's the night before to help her get the turkey stuffed and in the oven. We cook such a big bird that Grandma can't lift it by herself. Dad's fun on these occasions. He doesn't have anything to prove to Grandma. She sees right through him. As the huge bird slips and slides around, laughter fills the air. I usually spend the night, to help Grandma get ready. The little house is so full with the extra table in the living room, TV trays scattered about. It's fun. We pull out her pretty china. The grownups get that. By the time we get to younger kids, everything's mismatched. They don't care. We always work right up to the last minute. As each family arrives, the women jump in.

This Thanksgiving, we are all gathered at Grandma's as usual. It's been a good day so far. Chairs pushed out from the table, everyone's bellies are full. The women begin the process of undoing the mess. The kids move outside. The boys have a ball game going. I have a comfy spot on the porch with a book, hoping to be lost to the cleanup. It's getting close to dusk. I hear Dad calling for me. He's already got a good buzz on, not a good time to argue. I'm told to gather up the boys...Uncle Vernon's gonna take us to feed the animals.

A feeling of dread floods my body. I tell myself there's no need to worry with all the boys along. I'm just gonna have to stay mixed in. I can't let him get me off by myself. We all pile into the cab of his truck. I have Sam on my lap anyway, just in case. We stop by our place on the way. I send Kenny to the rabbits and Sam to the dogs. I'm off to the barn. I manage to keep my distance from Uncle Vernon. Seeing Ginger makes the worry melt away. I quickly fill her in. That always makes me feel better. She gives me a playful poke with her nose and makes me giggle.

We all pile back in the truck. I tuck Sam back in the safe spot on my lap. By the time we get to their place, I begin to let my guard down a little. Everything feels normal enough. I'm sure all my worry is nothing. It's been a while since he's tried anything. I haven't given him the chance. I've been sure to keep my distance. He sends the boys on to the barn and goes into the house to feed the dogs. I linger near the house, trying to keep Kenny and Sam in my sight.

Uncle Vernon bought a new saddle for our next season; he's been trying to get me excited about seeing it all day. I do really want to see it...just not with him, alone. They keep their tack down in the basement, so I decide to sneak around back and see if I can get a peek. My curiosity replaces my better judgment. No one I know has ever had a brand new saddle before. I'm sure whoever gets to show for him gets to use it. I turn the knob on the door, it opens easily. *No one ever locks their doors around here.* I sneak in; Uncle Vernon is right upstairs. Just want one quick look.

I turn on the light in the tack room, and there it is! Brand new! I'm drinking in the smell of the new leather; my eyes scan the intricate hand tooling. It's beautiful. As I run my hands over the stitching and the design etched in the leather, I'm startled by the squeak of the door behind me. I feel as if the air has suddenly been sucked from the room. A shadow falls across the floor, spurring movement, I turn quickly.

Uncle Vernon stands in the doorway, "She sure is a beauty."

"Yeah", I hear myself say, "Really pretty."

My eyes are riveted to his hand as he turns the lock. Then back to his face. His stance is unassuming, like Mister Rogers. Except for his eyes. His eyes say something different. More talk about the saddle as he's walking closer. The distance between us is diminishing by the second. My mind starts ticking through my options. I can't get out down here; the door's locked. If I can get past him fast enough, there's a door at the top of the stairs. He's big, but I can out run him. I'm inching my way to the stairs. Then his hands are on me. His lips…

Just as I'm about to leave my body, Tigua appears. He's never been here, on this side. With a steady glare, he roars, "It's time, June. You know what to do. You need to stay here and use what we have taught you. Remember what it feels like to be me, June. Remember the power you felt. I'm here with you. Become me."

With that, I close my eyes and focus intently on Tigua, remembering what it felt like to be the panther. I can feel his power enter my body. Sending clear signals to Sam of my danger, I start fighting. My body feels lithe and agile. Sam hears my call and is going from door to door, yelling my name. Kenny's not far behind. Their cries are getting more anxious with each pound.

With panther dexterity, I wiggle free and make my way to the staircase. He's close behind. I take the steps two at a time, making my way to the upper door. I can feel him; the words have stopped. He seems totally unfazed by the chaos of the moment, except for the determined set of his jaw. I reach out for the knob, terror grips me as I realize he's locked this door, too. Sam's on the other side working the lock, calling my name. I'm banging from my side, calling, "Please, let me out."

Suddenly, his fingers curl around my ankle. He yanks me down the length of the stairs. My face bangs a step or two, arms flailing in an attempt to catch myself. He pulls me to my feet. The lock clicks, and Sam opens the door, eyes wide, "Are you all right?"

Vernon flashes his Mister Rogers smile, "Oh she's alright. Aren't you June? She just missed a step on her way up. Came tumbling all the way down. I tried to catch her but didn't get here fast enough."

Sam is completely unconvinced, but Vernon just smiles that same Mister Rogers smile. He slowly lets go of my arm and brushes his hair back into place. He moves to the locked basement door, and as he opens it, he gives me a warning glance that makes my blood run cold.

Sam takes my hand and guides me up the stairs. Out of the dark basement. Out in the open air. Deep breath. Fresh air.

On the ride back to Grandma's, I position myself in the cab next to the window, as far away from Vernon as possible. I catch a glimpse of myself in the side mirror, tears streaming over my scratched up chin. I look away quickly and wonder if anyone will notice. He already has a story. How can I go back in there? They don't know. I guess I just have to pretend like everything's fine. Like nothing happened while I was locked in the basement. Keep my mask firmly in place. *We just went to feed the horses.*

Back at the house, Sam's drawn off by the rest of the boys.

Vernon grabs my arm hard and whispers in my ear, "Everything's fine. Nothing happened. There's nothing to tell anyway. Keep quiet, do you hear me?" His eyes lock on mine, I nod.

He leaves me there, alone, in the street. I lock another door, store another secret. I summon myself to enter the movie where nothing fits together. I float around the rest of the evening as if in a daze. I am posed for pictures on the lap of my favorite uncle. My last shred of trust in people, my dreams shattered. My escape from this place... up in smoke now. The day's marked down in history, skinned up face and all. No one notices.

For once going home is welcomed. I need to be alone, to be able to think. This changes everything.

Maiden, mother, wise woman

Bob and I decide to confront Vernon in the beginning, too. He and Carol have recently moved to a neighboring town with his job. Carol's continually calling; she wants the four of us to hang out, have dinner. I'm not interested. It's sad, because Aunt Carol and I were always so close. It's hard to stay close when there are secrets. I'm tired of making excuses, so we invite Vernon down with the pretense of dinner. He wants to bring Carol.

"No, no," I say. "I have some things that I need your input on, confidentially."

All puffed up, he says, "Well sure. What time works?"

We agree on seven. The days and hours become pregnant with tension as the time approaches.

Then, the doorbell. Bob has me seated in a comfy chair to help me to relax. He gets the door and Vernon waltzes in. He's all smiles, until he realizes there's no smell of dinner in the air. He feels the tension in the room, no niceties come his way.

"Have a seat," Bob says; guiding him to the sofa across from me.

"What's going on here?" spouts Vernon.

The nerves in my stomach push the words out like bile, "Vernon, I have been having trouble with some things. I'm trying to make some sense out of what I remember."

He begins to fidget around on the sofa. "What's this? What's going on here?" He stands.

So does Bob.

"I think it would be wise for you to have a seat and hear what June has to say," he says.

Vernon sits right down. Not sure why, but he does. Bob seems to have that effect on these men. First Dad, now Vernon.

Gaining some confidence from Bob, I push on, "I just want you to understand: I remember. I remember the things that you did to me when I was a girl. I need you to know how much you hurt me."

He starts to interrupt.

Bob raises his hand, "You will get to talk when June has said everything she needs to say." He urges me to continue.

Vernon swallows his words.

"I trusted you. I looked up to you, like a father. You know how things were with Dad. I needed you. But you just fell in line. Why would you do that to me?"

"What do you mean? Nothing ever really even happened."

"You locked me in a basement. If it weren't for Sam, something really bad would have happened. He saved me. From you."

"But nothing happened," he looked to Bob in order to gain a comrade, "You know how it is. When they're young and...."

"No. I don't know how it is," Bob interrupts. "Not with little girls, I don't. I think it's time for you to leave." Bob looks at me and nods. The tears stream down my face. In that moment we both understand that I'm getting nowhere. I nod back as a signal that I'm finished.

"Find a way to keep Carol away. I don't want to see you anymore. I don't want to have dinner with you, and I don't want to share my holidays with you. They are my family. You don't belong there. You make the excuses from now on, or I will tell Carol."

With his mouth open, ready to respond, Bob pushes him out the door.

It doesn't matter though. He's always there. Every time I go home. There he is, sitting in my mother's house. No amount of talking will ever change that.

Mom explains, "I can't lose my only sister, plus all that talk will give Grandma a heart attack! Carol is her favorite. You don't want to give Grandma another heart attack? It would kill her."

Every Christmas, Thanksgiving, Birthday. I never told Carol.

I wonder if I would be expected to have dinner with a child molester or rapist if he was a stranger, expected to welcome my captor into my home, allow him around my children…. Somehow I don't think so.

Under the umbrella of *family*, is all harm is negated?

Horse represents a journey and teaches us to discover our own freedom and power

I get up early the morning after and hurry to sneak out in an effort to avoid a face-to-face with anyone. I feel nervous about last night and what will come. Images dance around in my head. *I have to get out of here. I can't pretend this morning.* I slip into my jeans. With a glance out the window, I see the ground has a nice dusting of snow. It's the first snow of the season; I better bundle up. A slight smile crosses my face, it's all I can muster this morning. I tiptoe through the house, boots in hand. Opening the door as quietly as possible, I step into my boots.

Ginger feels my agitation as soon as I walk out of the house. She knows instantly that I need away from here, fast. She throws her head around with a whinny and backs herself up to the old tree stump. I can't help but smile, even if I don't want to. I cover the distance between us with long strides, I hit the stump and land on her back in one smooth motion. I grab a handful of mane, and we're off.

Feeling the warmth of the animal beneath me relaxes me a little. Sitting back, I let my mind wander. Ginger knows the way. It's a beautiful morning. The trees are glistening in the sunlight, almost twinkling like a Christmas tree. The morning air's cold in my lungs. The weight begins to lift with the lightness of the air. The creek's up ahead. Ginger looks back over her shoulder to make sure I'm ready. She picks up speed. We're in flight. I can hear my laughter, spilling into the air in spite of myself. Today, it felt foreign, somehow. Up the embankment to my special spot atop the cliff. I slide off and land softly in the cottony snow. After giving her a good tight hug around the neck, I ask her to stay close.

"I don't really want to be alone today. Something awful happened last night, and I need to figure out what I'm going to do. I'm so scared," I tell her as I nuzzle my face in her coat. "I'm afraid I am going to lose everything, everything I love." Tears are streaming down my face.

I sense movement behind me and glance back to see a black tail moving above the brush. The mare's ears prick up. I urge her to stay very still with my touch. I can feel the adrenaline rushing through her veins. As the animal breaks through the entanglements into the clearing, I gasp. What a sight to behold. The contrast of his blue black coat against the backdrop of fluffy white snow is truly awesome. His green eyes mirror my pain.

"Tigua!"

He roars in greeting. Ginger backs up, startled. She has never met Tigua before. I stroke her gently and croon softly, "It's okay girl; it's just Tigua. We have been friends for a long time. I know he looks scary, but he's really not scary at all. I was really afraid the first time, too. I'm excited that you finally get to meet him."

As she begins to relax, Tigua approaches.

I quickly make the introductions, "Tigua, this is my friend Ginger."

He bows his head to her, respectfully.

"Thank you for helping me last night," I say softly.

Tigua purrs, "I am always with you, June; we are one. Do you understand that now?"

"I do," I reply as I look around. "Why are you here? In this place?"

"We have some things to talk about, June. You have to learn to stay here with your body. You are older now. Your environment is shifting. All new people and places. It's not smart to leave your body unattended, out in the open."

I seem to be slipping back and forth between worlds pretty easily these days. I can be almost anywhere. If I get anxious, if I feel fear, almost instantly...I am in the meadow.

"With your body comes the means of action. It must be valued and protected. You understand that in becoming me, we can take many different forms. Pay attention! What you need will come to you." He pauses for a moment to make sure I am understanding, then continues. "It's time for the battle to begin. It's time for you to face the things that are happening to you. It's time to understand who you are and what you have available. The powers are with you. Take charge now. Take the actions needed to protect your body and own your life."

All I can think about is the horses, Ginger.

"I'm going to lose a lot," I say as I look back over my shoulder at Ginger. "I'm not sure I can stand that."

"All good things come with a price, June. These changes will bring great things to you. You will know your strength and your courage. You will be free," Tigua answers.

"How can I live here without the horses? I'm going to lose the horses. Without Uncle Vernon...I have nothing," I begin to cry.

He purrs and nuzzles my chin with his muzzle, "I know. It's going to be tough for a while. Things will have to turn upside down for you to be set free. You will have to be strong, June, and present. You have to stay here with this. Use your tools. It's time to use what you've been taught and save yourself."

"What about Sam?"

Tigua hears the worry in my voice and reassures me, "You have to take care of you first. Then he will be safe."

"I can't leave him here," I begin to sob.

"Have faith, June. He will be taken care of. Now, it's time for you to set things in motion. Only you can do it."

"Where do I start?" I ask.

"Deal with what's right in front of you first, the rest will follow. You have the power. I have to go back now. Know that I'm always with you. We are one, June, remember. Be careful of the slumber that takes people here. Remember what you know."

With that, Tigua saunters back toward the wood. I feel the weight of what I have to do as I watch him disappear from sight.

Atop my perch on the cliff, thoughts tumble around. I need a plan that allows me to keep up my work with the horses and keep Ginger. I can't lose her.

I can hear the echo of Tigua's words ringing through my head. *Deal with what's in front of you.* That's pretty clear. The most imminent thing right now is Dad and his fists. I should start there. The show season is winding down, so that leaves some space between me and Vernon. I can duck and weave for a while. One thing at a time.

I dream of being far, far away from here. I dream of me and Sam having a little place of our own. No them! Curtains on the windows. I can paint the rooms in happy, cheery colors. My dreams come to a halt with the realization that I don't even have a car. I can't go far without a car. I'm still in high school, no money. I've been working for a grocery part time, hoarding away every penny, with a car in mind. I'm nowhere close.

Chinese symbol for father

Things get worse at home. Dad has begun to have these episodes. He wanders around saying and doing really odd things. If we don't understand and respond correctly, he gets really angry. It's almost as if he's sleep walking, trapped inside a crazy dream. I find him one night late, frying Hi-Ho crackers in a skillet on the gas stove. He is irate because the "God damn turkey's bad." I try to calm him and turn the gas off. He turns on me, hitting me in the head hard enough that my plastic head band breaks, leaving pieces embedded in my scalp.

These episodes add a whole new level of unpredictability to our household. His visits to my room are equally bizarre. He's told me all sorts of things, called me every name that you can imagine: whore, tramp, slut, bitch. *I haven't even had a boyfriend; no one's ever touched me but you guys.* He sits on the floor with his back against the door, his preferred way of trapping me while he spews his crazy talk.

He told me once that he had a piece of paper saying that he was crazy.

"I can kill all of you if I want to," he says. "Not much would happen to me; just end up on some psych ward or something. It wouldn't be so bad. Might kinda like it. Wouldn't have to worry about all your shit."

"But why would you want to do something like that, Dad?"

His reply simple, he shrugs his shoulders, "Don't know, but I could." His head droops to his chest.

One afternoon, the house is empty. The boys are outside. I can't get the crazy paper out of my mind. What kind of paper gives someone the right, the right to kill with no consequences? I decide it's time to go on a treasure hunt. I need to see it. I need to touch it, to know what I'm dealing with. I rush up the stairs to my parents' room. I don't want to get caught up here. He keeps the guns in the closet. We're not supposed to go in there.

Secrets.

At the bottom of the closet under stacks of miscellaneous stuff I come across a metal box. Not a pretty box like Mom's, just a plain metal box, like a tool box. It opens easily. There's the house mortgage, marriage license…. At the very bottom I come face to face with the document. It's from the army. Section Eight discharge papers for reasons of…*insanity??* I can't believe it. It's weird that he would have kept something like that, even weirder that he told me about it. Things are coming to a head. I'm not sure what to expect. I have to be ready for anything. I slip the paper back in the box and get out of there as quickly as I can.

Another secret.

The panther possesses the medicine of shape shifting...the ability to shift their physical form to that of a two legged creature, or another creature, then back to their original form

High school. I have a lot going on in my head these days. Dad wanting to kill us, Randy and Uncle Vernon...I stay to myself. It's been hard for me to stay focused, pay attention. At the drop of a hat, I can be someplace fun hanging out with Tigua or the Teacher. Tigua has warned me about leaving my body alone, but I can't seem to help it. I seem to be there more than here. I have trouble talking to people. I don't know what to say. *What you need will come to you.*

I met Mr. Starling on my first day of High School. He is the school counselor, on top of teaching civics and psychology. I've got him for civics this year and civics is boring. With the ever present problems at home, my mind often wanders away during class. After calling attention to it a few times in front of everyone, he puts his counselor's hat on and calls me into his office.

"June, I've noticed that you're having trouble paying attention in my class."

I sit very still. No response.

"Is there some problem that we should talk about?"

I shake my head no.

"Well I want you to know if you ever have anything that you would like to talk to me about, my door is open.... Now pay attention in class. No more zoning out, okay?"

Mr. Starling is really handsome. All of the girls think so. Most of our teachers are women, and the few men we do have are old. Not Mr. Starling. He's a small wiry guy with dark, almost black hair that hangs on the collar of his brightly colored shirts, almost touching his shoulders. His mustache is huge, sort of like one of those old cowboys in the westerns that Dad watches. He even wears jeans to school. He's pretty cool for a teacher.

During semesters I don't have him for class, he asks me to be his assistant. Bit by bit, I begin to trust him. On a few occasions after particularly rough nights at home, I decide to share some of Dad's erratic behavior. I am careful not to expose any more than necessary, focusing mainly on Dad, leaving out the parts where any of us get tangled up with him. I balance my fear with the value of feedback from someone with an educated perspective, a psychology degree.

Mr. Starling has recently returned from a stint in the war. He shares the reoccurring nightmares that haunt him, opening the door for more sharing. My dreams often haunt me. He understands, after getting to know me, that zoning out was not what was going on. He also knows that it isn't safe for me to be leaving my body vacant so often, especially out in public. People make fun of me all the time about it. Not that I care that much. I am completely unaware, in trance, when a spit ball or something worse comes sailing across the room aimed directly at my head. Teachers tend to frown upon these classroom disturbances. Mr. Starling has taken it upon himself to keep me here, in this place. It seems everywhere I turn, he's there, pulling me back. He never touches me, just some small noise or a feeling of his presence.

I recently made the cheerleading squad. It's a weird thing for me, but I thought it might be a good way to make some friends. I have really never been too interested in sports. I went to Sam's little league games, but I was watching Sam. I didn't care about the game. We have to learn all the rules to all the games—basketball, football, volley ball, even wrestling. There's even a class. I passed, but I still don't get it.

I'm standing on the sidelines. All ten of us in a row. I've taken my usual spot on the end. It's been a good game by the looks of the scoreboard. The crowd seems to be having a great time. Everyone is worked up. It seems as if we have been saying the same few words over and over for a really long time. "Go, Go, Go, Go Raiders go." It lulled me right off. I'm standing in the meadow looking around for Tigua when I hear faintly, way off in the distance, "June, J..U..N..E." I turn and look behind me, no one is there. I brush it off and begin meandering up the path when I hear it again….

"June! June, they are leaving you; you need to go."

I look around again. Still no one. Then there's this big clap. I am back in my body, startled. Mr. Starling is yelling for me to hurry, pointing to center court. The whole squad is in formation, waiting… for me.

Junebug teaches us to navigate different realms bringing forth opportunities to recycle, reinvent and repurpose what you have and know, in how you think and act

Dad's home from work when we get off the bus. I can feel the pit form in my stomach as we come around the curve and I see his truck in the drive. It's been such a good day at school. Maybe he'll be in an okay mood. If we can just get past him to change clothes. That's the tricky part; the bedrooms are situated at the back of the house down a long skinny hall. There's no way out if he follows us back there.

Gathering Sam's hand in mine, we make our way down the drive. Kenny's not far behind. It's about a quarter mile to the house from the bus. With each step, we worry what we might walk into. He's not usually here at this time of day. I wonder what's going on. We usually get a couple of stress-free hours before he gets home. On top of that, Mom's not here; that's not good. Not that it makes that much difference, but a little. At least he's aware, on some level that someone is watching. Alone, he has free reign.

"Stay out of the way and keep quiet. Head straight back and grab some clothes. We can change in my room," I tell Sam.

He nods his head, real serious like. We enter the house. Dad's in the kitchen cooking dinner. He does like to cook and seems to be in a good mood. He's smiling, anyway. The three of us look on skeptically.

"How was school?" he says in our direction.

Different plan. Get dressed and go outside and start on your chores.

He looks up at me nervously.

I send him off with a nudge.

I reply with a "good" and hope to be able to just keep on walking.

"Well," he says, "the kid has a good day but has nothing to say about it." He's standing like Peter Pan with his hands on his hips.

He's acting like he wants to hear about my day. I'm caught a little off guard.

I stop, turn his way, gather myself up and start talking, "We're doing this really cool project on the solar system." I don't really like science that much, but I love the stars. Once I get going, the words just start spilling out.

"...and we're learning about all of the planets. Mars is the second smallest planet. Mercury is the smallest. Mars is the red planet. It's because of the iron oxide. It was named after the Greek god of war..."

Suddenly he stops me; he's found some fault with my information, "It was the Roman god. Mars was named after the Roman god of war." My Dad reads everything that's not nailed down. Even though he quit school in the tenth grade, he didn't stop learning. He knows every word in the dictionary, every fact in the encyclopedia. He even knows what page every word is on. He has a photographic memory. I watched him have a priest turned upside down over words in the Bible. He'd only read it once. So, it's not smart to disagree with him over science facts. It's not smart to disagree with him period, but I still haven't learned how to keep quiet.

I'm sure that what I'm saying is right, then, "but that's what the teacher said" comes out. It is a stupid thing to say, and I know it. I've been down this road before. For some reason it sends him into a rage for me to bring up a teacher.

"I don't give a shit what that God damn teacher said! That's a bunch of bullshit."

The words start to pile up in my throat. I really like my science teacher this year. He's pacing around, getting more agitated with each step. He throws the towel that has been across his shoulder on the ground. I can feel the force of the air first, his huge hand heading right towards my head. He doesn't have to worry about the bruises if he hits me in the head. I try to hang with my body, remembering Tigua's words. He told me I need to, but after a particularly hard blow, I feel myself rising up.

I see Kenny in the doorway of the kitchen. I hadn't noticed him when I was down there. From above, I watch Kenny inching closer, working his way to the fringe, watching. I notice the tension in his muscles, the clench of his jaw, his stance, as if he's ready to jump in. His face is full of pain.

I'm curled in the fetal position with my father kicking me, the point of his boot digging into my thighs, my ribs, yanking my hair. I come in to get a closer look. I focus in on Kenny. I sense the helplessness he feels. He's just watching, not able to do anything. The inward battle with his thoughts...*Can I take him?* He knows that he can. It's the after. What happens after you fight your Dad? He is stronger than Dad, he knows it; and Dad knows it too. But how do you fight your Dad? He's just a kid.

Dad's recent obsession has been to make Kenny feel little. Every year on Kenny's birthday comes the annual arm wrestling contest. In front of everybody, Kenny has *let* Dad win for the last couple of years, but this year, at the very last second, he did it. He made the choice to take him. Confusion overtook Dad's face. Lots of bluster over letting Kenny win. Things changed after that, though. From that point on, it's been about the words and they hurt just as bad. Dad's a master with words; he knows just where to stick that knife and just how to turn it. *Kenny has to be beaten down to size.* In the end, he's more afraid of the words...and of tomorrow. He has no choice but to keep quiet and watch. Watching's hard, in a way, harder than being the one getting hurt. Guilt comes with watching.

I'm pulled back down as Dad's yanking on my arm, telling me to get up. I'm back in. With full awareness, I gather myself up and rise to my feet. Resolute, I throw my shoulders back and look him square in the eye. Not a tear.

He backs away.

I find my way to the barn to think. I climb to my spot in the loft; up on a bale or two, my mind works its way back to Kenny. He feels so much pain. He always acts so mean and tough. I never thought of him feeling anything but anger. I just never really thought about him much at all. I never thought about what it would feel like to watch with no escape to the other side. He's just a boy. **Boys don't fight their Dads.** That's the unspoken rule. He thinks that maybe he can take him. Somehow this insight into Kenny gives me courage. The boys are getting hurt too—Kenny with his weight of guilt and Sam with his ulcers. I have to stop it. I have to.

I'm the only one who will.

Reclaiming one's own true power

I know it won't be long before my new found strength will be tested. Things have become even more precarious than normal. The liquid gold intake is up high. Dad's getting into trouble at work over anger issues. He has been rewarded for his ability to go from ninety to nothing in an instant in his new position as union representative. The position consists of fighting and arguing, right up his alley. Even with that, he's been over the top. He thinks no one knows, but I do. Bottles are hidden everywhere, his special spot being the tank behind the toilet. I guess it stays nice and cold there. There are lots of trips to the bathroom. He also has a bottle hidden behind the seat in the cab of his truck and a few in the barn. I'm sure he's been sneaking out to his truck during the day to add a little nip to his constant cup of coffee. He seems to be well on his way to a drunken stupor by the time he gets home from work.

This evening I don't move quickly enough, or don't read his thoughts in anticipation of his needs—whatever the reason, he has me pinned up against the refrigerator, his fist cocked back, ready. Mean, hateful things are spewing from his lips.

Tigua appears over his shoulder. "Remember, June," are the only words he speaks.

With that, he leaps right into my body. I can feel his strength well up inside. My muscles feel tense and ready to spring. With determination and resolution, I look my father directly in the eye.

I challenge him with my demeanor, "Go ahead, hit me, but think about it hard. I'm done. No more. I will have you thrown in jail. No crazy farm for you. You will spend the rest of your life in prison, if I start talking."

He looks at me intently as he weighs my words. I can see the wheels turning in his head as he's trying to decide if I have what it takes to really do it. I'm shaking with rage and fear, knees weak. Either he'll back down, or he's going to kill me.

The seconds it took for him to process the situation seem to last an eternity. He brings his fist in close to my face. So close that I can feel the heat coming off of his hand. He doesn't hit me. He hits the fridge instead. He takes a step back, cursing under his breath, "*God damn kid.*" He walks away, muttering. When I can compose myself and look around, I realize that we have an audience. Mom and Kenny stand there, stunned.

As I walk past my mother, she grabs my arm. Looking me square in the eye, she says, "I knew that one day, you would be strong enough to stand up to him."

I stare right back, and jerk my arm away. On my way to the door, I say, "It's not like *you're* going to do anything." The power of the panther is still rushing through me like a tidal wave. I need to get outside, out from under their roof, out from under the looming doom.

Ah, fresh air. I breathe it in, filling my lungs to their capacity. I wonder how things are going to play out. Without me as a punching bag, what will it be like around there? Sitting in my spot atop the hay bales, I begin to work on a plan. No more waiting.

Readiness, steadfastness and hardiness

Today, Mr. Starling has on his counseling hat. We have been spending time together looking at colleges. He knows that things are tough at home and is trying to help me find a way to be able to afford it on my own. He knows I won't be getting any help from my parents. Scholarships are definitely in the cards; I have always been a good student.

He's going to be disappointed with what I need to talk to him about today. As I sit across from him, I struggle to find the words. He has put so much time and effort into me. There's nothing to do but just start talking.

"Mr. Starling, I have sort of changed my mind about what I need to do."

"What do mean?" he asks.

"Well, I am thinking about beauty school."

"What?" He's stunned.

I take in a big breath and continue on, "Things aren't good at home, not good at all. I'm going to need a way to provide for me and Sam. I need money fast. I've been spending time at the Cut and Curl, watching. I'm sure I can do it. I've been practicing on my friends and already have gotten a few referrals from people. I work on them

148

in the kitchen at home. It takes less than a year, and then maybe we can get away from here."

His eyes are filled with compassion. He knows how badly I wanted to continue on with school. My dreams of a psychology degree are floating downstream. He understands how much energy it has taken to get to this place, how much I am giving up.

"I don't see any other way," I explain. I'm sure he can hear the resignation in my voice.

He switches gears and dives into finding me the best beauty school in the metropolitan area. The plan is put in motion. He even offered to help with the student loan paper work, knowing if he doesn't no one will. Leaving the office, I smile to myself. There is one kind man on the planet. If things can just hold out for the months it will take to get through beauty school....

Now it's time for the rest of my plan. I need a car. The school we decided on is in the city. I only know one way to come up with the money quickly. It's time to have that talk with Ginger. I am dreading it.

Horse symbolizes the journey towards one
discovering their own freedom and power....
Their clairvoyance gives them the ability
to recognize those with mystic abilities

I decide we could both use a nice ride before the hard stuff, for
old time's sake. In the feed lot, I find Ginger taking an afternoon
nap. I begin talking softly; I don't want to sneak up on her.
That's never fun, getting startled from a nice rest. I know about that
from experience. As she stirs, I stroke her gently.

"Hey, sweet girl," I croon, "You want to go play for a while?"

Ginger never turns down a romp through the woods. I throw
a halter on her. She backs up to the familiar stump. I climb on
bareback. I want to feel her beneath me, the warmth of her body,
that connection, the connection that is only ours. It might be one of
the last times. Winding our way through the trees, I become aware
of all the sounds. I can hear the small animals scurrying from our
path, leaves rustling, birds singing in the trees. Everything seems so
happy. They don't know what I have to do. They don't understand
that our adventures are coming to an end.

A tear leaks from my eye. *I can't start crying.* I wipe it away quickly and begin to talk about anything I can think of. Anything other than what's hanging in the air. In the guise of protecting Ginger, I'm pulling out all the stops to distract myself. Ginger glances back over her shoulder, making sure I'm hanging on tight as she begins to pick up speed. I lean in close in preparation for the creek...flying. Will I ever feel this again? I need to savor it, store away the feeling. Will I ever have a connection with another living being like we have now? I push the thoughts from my mind as the familiar feeling in my belly takes center stage. It never lasts quite long enough, the feeling of being suspended in air, as if time stops for a second. If only I could stop time just long enough for us to disappear.

The sound of the leaves crunching as we touch down on the other side makes me smile, in spite of the situation. Keeping up our momentum, we quickly find ourselves at the top of the hill, the cliff up ahead. I throw my leg over Ginger's head and slide off, landing softly in the cushion of the thick grass. Ginger drops her head and begins enjoying her snack. A sad smile flitters across my face. What will I say? *Oh, by the way, sorry Ginger. We have had lots of fun, but I'm trading you in for a new car.* It sounds pretty lame, but it's true. Pushing away the inevitable for a time, I settle into my customary spot on the cliff. The air filled with the looming dread. The strength has drained from my body. It just isn't fair. Not that I really expect fair, but this is too much. How can I put a price on my best friend? She is the one that has been there for me through thick and thin. No person has ever even come close to that in my world. Ginger's the only one to take up for me. Dad and Vernon end up on their heads every time they try to get on her. She thinks they are both jerks. She's always there waiting for me at the stump when I need to escape fast. I lose control completely. The tears come in a torrent. I feel like a traitor.

I close my eyes for a moment to catch my breath. Sensing a presence above me, I open my eyes to the Teacher. He reaches for my hand and helps me to my feet. He draws me into a comforting embrace. Wrapping my arms around him, I snuggle my face into his chest and allow my emotions free reign. As my tears begin to ebb, the Teacher takes my chin and lifts my face. His look is full of compassion. The locked up words begin to spill from my lips.

"This is too much. I can't do this. This is worse than all of the rest put together. She has been such a true friend to me. She knows just what I need. She helps me get away. She knows what he does to me. No one else knows, just her. I need someone to know, to know it all. I can't bear losing her." Running out of breath with the gush, I pause.

The Teacher pats my back, and gently leads me to a soft place in the grass, beneath a grand old oak tree. Sitting cross-legged before me, he says, "June, things are always changing. The universe is in constant motion. You are a fast learner, a prize pupil; your world is spinning and changing faster than most. The scenery needs to change for the game to progress. Pain comes in resisting. Things can't stay the same and change at the same time."

I nod my head in understanding. "It still hurts."

"I know, little one. Your friend has other work to do now, too. Her work with you is done. You are at a fork in the road, and it is time for the two of you to go your separate ways. You can't cling to the past and expect anything to change," I know he's right, but I don't like it.

As if reading my thoughts, he adds, "It doesn't mean that what you have to do is going to be easy, but out of the pain good things will grow. Find your strength, June. Call on the powers available to you. You have everything you need in here," He points to the place where my heart is held. "Clinging will only bring the slumber. Be careful of the slumber."

With that, his image begins to fade. Using everything I can muster, I push myself to a standing position and slowly take the few steps, closing the distance between me and Ginger. She's still enjoying her afternoon snack, her head buried in the grass. I fight back the tears that threaten to spill over as I stroke her face.

"You have some special work to do with another family," I talk through a giant lump in my throat. "Maybe you will be lucky and the little girl will have a nice daddy this time. They might even have a real barn with stalls where you can get in out of the rain and snow. And maybe some pasture of your own, you can just graze whenever you want. That would be nice. The little girl might even like to fly as much as I do. Maybe they will even have a creek…. I have to buy a car, Ginger," I choke. "I am so sorry! I have to get Sam away from here, sweet girl."

The tears. I share all that the Teacher has told me. Ginger shows understanding by nuzzling me with her nose. We both know now what has to be done. I glance around, taking in my beloved space. I know somehow, this too, is part of the changing scenery, a chapter closing. We take the ride home slowly. The sparkle has faded from my beloved woods. There's no flying over our creek. The cloud is heavy over both of us, as if everything around us has joined in our mourning. The quiet engulfs us. There are no leaves crunching. The birds have stopped singing. The leaves are even drooping on our trees, as if waving goodbye, as if knowing we will never cross this path again.

Chinese symbol for father

In Dad's world, there's a strict set of rules that he lives by. They aren't everyone else's rules, but they are his. If I buy the car with my own money, it's mine. He won't touch it. No taking my keys. If he puts one dime in, he's part owner and will have say so. Approaching him with selling my horse has to be strategic. There's a fifty/fifty chance he'll consider the money his. I might lose Ginger for no reason. I have to catch him in just the right mood with just the right amount of the liquid gold in the hatch. I need him to remember. I figure with what I've saved along with the tack and the sale of Ginger, I'll have enough. I've had a conversation with one of Dad's friends, Tom. He owns a used car lot. He said he would help me find something. He's one I kind of trust. He has a couple that he thinks will be good. After looking them both over, my favorite hands-down, is a pearly, sky blue mustang with white leather interior. Ironic, trading a live horse for a metal one. It seems God has a way of playing these little tricks, to see if I'm paying attention.

Having a car already picked out will help my case, for sure. Dad loves cars, especially cool cars. He's going to like the idea of the Mustang. My plan is to get him all caught up in the details and gloss over the money part without much notice. That's my plan. I do my research, learn all that I can about the stuff that boys pay attention to, like the engine size, horse power. I'm hoping to impress him a little. I ask Tom to put the figures in writing so that I won't get confused when Dad starts grilling me. I borrow my mother's Polaroid and ask Tom to take a snap shot of me standing next to the Mustang. Ready, set, go.

He loves the car in spite of himself. I can read it on his face, though his mind moves quickly to the money. "Where you gonna get the money? You can't afford something like this," he says. I quietly show him the figures Tom has written down for me.

He's impressed with the deal, "But, I'm still not sure where you're gonna get the money,"

My eyes instantly drop to the floor, "I thought I'd sell Ginger." I got it out without tears. The tears will send this in a different direction instantly. Dad hates tears, so I move on quickly. "With what I've saved working, and the money from selling Ginger and my tack, I should have enough. I have to be able to get back and forth to school, Dad."

"What about all the money I've spent feeding the damn thing?"

"I appreciate all you've done for us, but I won't be able to go to school without a car."

"You're going to throw your job away at the Kroger?"

I recently got promoted to checkout clerk.

"You're in the union now. Make a good life."

"I will be good at this. It won't cost you anything. I'll work as much as I can. I have student loans for the tuition. Please," I beg.

For some reason, after eyeing me up, he agrees, "I'll put an ad in the paper this week." The next stage of my plan is in motion.

Change and mortality

Ginger gone, car in the drive. Emotions are stirred up. There's no one to talk to, to tell my deepest secrets. The metal horse, lots of fun too. The scenery is changing. After finally standing my ground with Dad, it seems things have calmed down at home for a second.

Money is at an all-time low for me. I thought things at home might be stable enough to move in with a new friend from beauty school. She lives in the city, not too far from the school. Gas is eating me alive driving the forty five miles back and forth every day. I decide to run the plan past Mom. I'm trying to gauge if Sam's gonna be okay here without me.

"Hey, Mom, can I talk to you for a sec?" I guide her into the kitchen and take a seat at the table indicating for her to do the same. "Gail's mom has invited me to stay with them during the week. I can save some money on gas and come home on the weekends and work."

"He will never go for that," she says, shaking her head vigorously.

"I really don't care. I need to do this or I don't know how I'll be able to stay in school. I need to know that you and Sam will be okay."

"I can't live here without you, June."

"You're going to have to, Mom. Sam needs you. I won't always be here. You knew this day would come sometime. I have to do this. I can't work enough to pay for the gas."

Together, we decide it's worth a shot. I throw a few things in a bag, grab my tooth brush and try to get the stuff packed in the car before Dad notices. I put the suit case in the back seat and close the door. I take a big deep breath. I might actually get away with it. Excitement at the possible freedom begins to tingle in my belly. I'm gonna get out of here before he notices. Just as I'm pulling open the driver door, he shows up out of nowhere and grabs my arm, spinning me around to face him.

"Where do you think you're going?"

My mind races, searching for the perfect words, "Well, Dad I'm having some money trouble, and I thought I'd stay with a friend in the city for a while to save on gas."

"What? You think you're leaving, moving up there?"

"I thought I would, yeah, just during the week, though. I'll be home on the weekends so I can work. I can't really afford not to do this, Dad."

"You're not going anywhere."

"I'm gonna have to drop out of school if I stay here."

"Not my problem, you're not going," he's getting more agitated by the minute. The pressure on my arm is increasing.

"I really need to do this."

He steps back, glaring at me. I can tell he's thinking, weighing it out. "Well, I'll tell you what. If you do this, if you leave this house, you will never see Sam again. I will take him and leave, and you will never find us. Leave the country if I have to. You or your mother, you will never see him again."

"You can't do that."

"You watch me."

The bile rises in my throat. I can't let that happen under any circumstances. I unload my car, shoulders sagging. I guess it means I'm working every minute I'm not in school. I'm back in town in the evenings by about six thirty. I can just head straight there. I'll be done before long, only a few months left. I'll just ask for more hours at work.

I can't quit school or we'll never get out of here.

Celtic symbol for mother

I can go to Grandma's anytime I want, now that I have wheels. I show up there sometimes in the middle of the night. I pull into the drive and summon my nerve. *I'm gonna tell her this time. Maybe she can help me get out of here.* I gently take Chi-Chi down from her favorite perch on my shoulder and set her in my lap. Take the keys from the ignition and sit there. I'm not sure how long, mindlessly stroking Chi-Chi. Finally, I open the car door. With her in my arms, we walk slowly down the drive. I can feel Grandma stir with the squeak of the old metal gate. I inch my way up the sidewalk and maneuver the few steps up onto the porch through the dark, thick night. As my hand reaches for the old screen door, she's already pushing it open from the other side. Each time, always the same, she imediately pulls me in and throws her arm around me, leading me into the house. She guides me into her bedroom. It's so late, we don't want to wake all the kids. We take our seats on the edge of the her bed, her arm still around my shoulder.

"What is it Junebug. What's happened?"

No matter how hard she tries to get me talking, I just sit there, not a word. *How can I tell her? What if I cause her to have a heart attack like Mom warns?* Rocking back and forth, staring at the floor, Chi-

Chi still in my arms. In the end, I stand and look into her eyes for the first time…. ***If she even for a second thought…*** No I can't risk it.

"I better get back now. I need to get back; Sam needs me. He has school tomorrow."

"Why don't you just stay here till morning? Get some rest, and I will get you up really early."

I'm already shaking my head no, "I have to get home to Sam."

"What has happened? Has something happened, June?"

I have to get home. If Dad wakes up and finds me gone, he might take Sam away. I reach for her and hug her tight, "I just have to go, Grandma. Thank you. I love you so much."

She tries to stop me. She tries to get me to tell her why the terror is in my eyes. I won't. It's the after that's so scary. What happens after you talk out loud about these horrible things?

What happens…tomorrow?

She gives us the ability to reinvent oneself

O
utside of the few excursions with the family, I'd never been to the city, not by myself. It's big, and loud, and more than a little intimidating. I've been with the same people all my life. On one hand, I am naive and innocent, while on the other I have more life experience than most my age. An interesting combination. My exposure to the outside world has been at a minimum. Now there are new people, new sights, and new thoughts, everywhere. It's kind of scary, but I love it. Most of all, I love the new thoughts. This fabulous older man from Germany owns the school. I've never met anyone from another country before or spoken to anyone with an accent. I have to work hard to understand. Taken by my innocence and my innate abilities, I've become his prize pupil. I feel like a sculptor working with an ever moving modality. The challenge of putting in a shape that will hold in spite of the person wearing it. Wearable, mobile art. I thrive in this environment under his guidance.

I encounter ways of life that I have never even considered before, number one being homosexuality. I've heard the words "gay" and "fag" thrown around high school by the boys. I thought they were just words. Now here I am; I've met two, and they just up and announced it to everyone. Terry even wears make-up. Disarming them with my ever-present string of questions, we have become fast friends. I understand, in my core, the feeling of always living on the fringe of the rest of the world; it seems we operate from the same plane. Its lots of fun to shop with them. I don't have any money, but its still fun to watch the boys flit around ogling everything in sight, often in the girls' department. Our laughter fills the store. It feels good and helps me forget for a while. I still have to go home, but while I'm here I can pretend to be someone else. Someone who's fun and happy. Nobody knows me here. They don't know him. This is a dimension of my life where he adds no color. Here I can push it away and soak up everything around me. I'm here without any of them. No one knows what I'm doing or thinking.

Mr. Hundel has an apprenticeship lined up for me after graduation. One problem: it's in the city. I really need to be closer to home. Sam's showing signs of my not being around much. He's been sick a lot lately, and school isn't going so well. Mr. Hundel really thinks it would be a good step for my career. I would have the opportunity to work under someone for a while who has been really successful in the industry. I could learn a lot by being in that environment.

There's also a position at home. An established barber wants to take his place unisex. It isn't a hard decision, really. Sam wins out easily and I take the job back home. When my new boss went to school they weren't trained in any of the chemicals of the business, like color and perms. He's trying to do them anyway, and not well! On the other hand, he can really cut hair. He's good. We have a lot to learn from one another. I will be here for Sam, and the money I save on gas will be a bonus. Decision made.

*Symbolizes strength through unity as
well as the importance of being prepared*

W e get past Christmas without incident; New Year's Eve's
right around the corner. My friends are trying to talk
me into having a party. Together, Mom helps me come
up with a plan. Secrets. Dad can't know. My parents have plans to
go to a party in the city. Mom has a new boss, Harold. His daughter
is having the party. Mom's new job, ironically, is managing the only
liquor store in town. They are planning to leave around seven and
my guests should arrive around seven thirty. Mom's supposed to call
before they start their trip home from the city. This gives me time
to clear everyone out and get the place in order, no telltale signs. My
friends understand the balancing act that's involved in maneuvering
around Dad. There are ten or eleven of us pretty equally divided
between girls and guys. They're really good with Sam. He's kind of
become the mascot. It's not always the best environment for him,
but we try. He has fun.

Parents gone, my friends begin arriving with their coolers in
tow. There's a spread of snacks on the counter, and I already have
the music blaring. The boys are looking forward to a night of poker
and beer; the girls dancing and gossip. I sneak a sip of Sam's drink

periodically just to make sure. Kenny is downing his share of the beers. We pulled it off; everyone's having a really good time.

Then the phone rings. I look at the clock. It's too early for Mom to be calling. Then the pit starts to form in my stomach. I quiet everyone and pick up the phone, the familiar dread sweeps through me. Mom's words come out in a rush. I'm having trouble understanding.

"Your Dad's on his way home. Get the boys and the guns and get out of there. He wants to kill me."

"Wait, What? Slow down Mom, I can't understand what you're saying."

"June, something terrible has happened. Your father thinks I'm having an affair. He put Frank in the hospital."

"Frank, who's Frank?"

"He's just a friend of one of Harold's girls. It doesn't matter, June. Just listen, stop with the questions," she begins to cry now. "June, you have to hurry. He just left. He's coming there to get a gun. You have to pack up all the guns and get out of there. Who knows what he might do if he sees you. Now go!"

The line goes dead. I'm left standing there holding the phone, speechless, my mind racing. Knowing this time would come was one thing; it actually being here, completely different. I gather myself together and put the phone back in its cradle. Adrenaline takes over, and I sprint into action. I find Kenny, oblivious and doing quite well at the poker table. I whisper the need to speak with him. Typical of Kenny, he has no interest; he's winning. My voice rises, making the underlying terror transparent.

Without any further argument, he leaves the table and follows me to my bedroom. I replay the phone call for him, "I don't know, Kenny; the booze, the guns, and the crazy paper...we might be in for some trouble."

"Crazy paper? What do you mean?"

I quickly share the story of how I found the paper and Dad's ramblings of killing us.

"Not good. Where should we go?" Kenny's fighting to keep his growing panic at bay as he sits heavily on the edge of the bed. "I should have taken him when I had the chance," he mutters.

I take a seat beside him and put my arm around his shoulder. Odd for us; we rarely touch. We sit in mutual silence for a minute. When I feel that we've wasted all the time we dare on sentiment, I breathe deep and begin talking aloud through our options.

"He will look at Grandma's first."

"We can't let him go up there like this," Kenny says.

"I know, she's got three little ones up there right now. What if he gets a hold of a gun somehow? We can't put them in the middle of all this. She needs to be able to meet him at the gate with the truth. Grandma won't lie; he knows that. We can't give him a reason to go in the house; she just can't know anything. She can't protect us now, anyway."

"What about Uncle Clarence?" Kenny suggests.

"I don't know. He's pretty scared of Dad. He'll take us in, but he'll also let Dad in. I hate it, but the least likely place would be Uncle Vernon's. He's not intimidated by Dad at all. He's liable to meet him in the drive with a shot gun."

Kenny looks at me for a moment, then, "Do you think he'll let us stay?"

"Not sure, but we don't really have any other options that I can see. Dad knows I've been keeping my distance from Vernon. Hopefully their place won't even be on his radar."

Kenny knows what a pride swallowing choice this is for me. He remembers the basement and draws me into one of his rare embraces.

Twice in a just few minutes: funny what fear does. We're on the same team now with a common goal. Survival. Vernon and Carol were also at the party. They should be on their way home, too. First priority: the guns.

"Do you know where he hides the guns?"

Kenny nods.

"Okay. Why don't you get the guns and lock them up in the trunk of my car. While you're doing that, I'll make up some excuse and get everybody out of here."

My friends feel something in the air and have already put the house back in order. They are slipping into their coats when we resurface. I tell them a version of the truth in an effort to push the dwindlers out the door. Just the bare bones of the story. I'm a terrible liar so I stick close to the truth. We need to get moving. I'm thankful to have the condition of the place off our minds. Dad doesn't need anything else added to his list of things to be pissed off about.

We are finally alone in the kitchen. Sam's eyes are full of questions but he's not saying a word. Fear is hanging in the air. Kenny and I lock eyes in understanding. He takes the stairs two at a time and begins the mission of taking charge of the guns. My job is to fill Sam in. I choose my words carefully in an effort to balance his need to know with the fear that I see creeping into his eyes.

"We are going to go stay at Uncle Vernon's tonight, Sam. Dad has kind of freaked out, and we don't want to be here when he gets back. It'll be fun anyway; you guys will have lots of fun playing." He's unconvinced. "You know you will. Now go throw some things in a bag. Grab enough for two or three days, and don't forget your tooth brush," I give him a hug. "Now hurry; we can talk more in the car." He runs off in the direction of his room without a word.

"How we doing Kenny?" I yell up the stairs.

"Found'em," comes back.

I run up the stairs to help him, "Do you have the keys?"

Again, Kenny nods.

After locking the guns safely in the trunk, we hurry back inside to gather some things for ourselves.

"How long do you think we'll be staying?"

"I told Sam two or three days. I'm not staying there any longer than that."

As we pull out of the drive, Kenny's watching out for Dad.

"Headlights around the curve, coming our way," he yells. "Hurry, just in case it's him."

"Is it?"

"I don't know. Hurry! Maybe we should pull in here for a second and see if it comes this way," Kenny says as he chews his bottom lip.

We pull off on a small gravel road down the highway a bit and turn off the headlights. And we wait. A car whizzes by. We look at each other and breathe.

"That wasn't him, right?" I ask.

"No, that was just a car. I think we're good. Let's go. Hurry!" We inch back onto the highway, "Keep the lights off until we can't see the house. We don't want to take any chances, just in case," Kenny says anxiously.

Vernon's house is way out in the country off of a dark gravel road. We'll be able to hear a car coming or see the lights. We decide it'll be better to park around back. The car will be harder to see from the road. We get there first, so we wait. Each of us dealing with our nerves in our own way. Me talking and laughing. Laughter in the place of tears. That's been a thing for a while. When I get scared or uncomfortable, I laugh. Inappropriate at times, like now. But there it is. Sam is in constant motion with a constant stream of words. Kenny just sits in silence, not moving a muscle; he's practicing his invisible thing.

"What do you think they're gonna say when they see us? Will they let us stay? People stay out of things like this, you know. If they don't want us to stay, we won't have a choice; we'll just have to go to Grandma's. If so, we'll just have to pray Dad's already been there," I chatter on. No response, none expected; we are each in our own bubble.

The sound of tires on the gravel, headlights in the distance. The air in the car goes suddenly heavy and sour. *Please God, don't let it be Dad.* I say the little prayer over and over in my head. As the sounds get closer, we realize it isn't Dad's truck. It sounds like Vernon. We wait just to be sure. We walk up to the house hand in hand, even Kenny. The adults don't seem too surprised to see us; it's as if they were expecting us. They hurry us inside, out of sight. Sam's sent off to play with his cousins for a while, leaving me and Kenny to figure out what the hell's going on. Aunt Carol busies herself with getting us settled. She seats us around the kitchen table, and we wait in silence while she makes us cocoa. With a big mug of hot chocolate on the table in front of us, we listen. We sit in silence, cocoa untouched, wide-eyed as she attempts to recreate the events of the evening, starting at the beginning.

"We were all having such a good time. She had her place decorated so cute. She still had her tree up. The furniture was kind of pushed back cause the dancing had started. Your Mom's just sitting on the couch talking with Frank, when, out of the blue, your Dad came up behind them in a rage, fists a flyin', accusing him of sleeping with your mother," she goes on. "Frank was blindsided, so your Dad is just pounding him. Your Mom dives to the floor. Things start flying.

Your Dad picks up a bottle of wine and throws it at Frank's head. Hit the Christmas tree instead, thank God," she pauses to take a breath and let it sink in a minute before she continues. "Frank gets away and is able to get outside, because Harold and Vernon are holding your Dad back."

Not sure whether to laugh or cry.

"He knocks Harold off balance. You know how scrappy your Dad is. He breaks free and flies out of the house after Frank, tackles him in the yard. Frank hits his head, blood everywhere. Your Dad has him pinned down; he's on top of him and starts hitting him again. I'm not sure how they finally got him calmed down enough to set Frank free," she says, taking another breath.

Kenny and I look at each other.

"Is he okay," I ask softly, "Frank, I mean?"

"I think so," Carol says. "Looked like maybe a broken jaw and there was the cut on his head, maybe a broken rib or two. They took him away in an ambulance. Your Mom begged him not to press charges. He said he wouldn't."

The pit in my stomach is growing.

"There's more; your Mom is having an affair," she says while moving some crumbs around on the table. She won't look at us. "But...It's not Frank."

"Who is it?" Kenny's jaw is set.

What? I thought I heard her say Harold.

Kenny sounds really far away, "Harold? Are you kidding? How long?"

"A while. She thinks she loves him."

"He's married, too," Kenny fumes.

I'm finally able to speak, "Oh God, this really isn't good. His wife's almost as unpredictable as Dad. This could get really ugly."

My aunt nods in agreement, head down. My fear turns into downright terror. There is potential for someone to lose their life here. He can always buy another gun.

"Why on earth would she talk this guy into not pressing charges? He can't kill anyone if he's in jail," I say quickly.

"I don't know," Carol says, her eyes down, head shaking.

Leaning up against the sink, Vernon listens. He doesn't say a word until Carol finishes. Then, "We all need to get some sleep. Things always look better in the morning. You know Kenny, he will undoubtedly be calmed down by morning and then we can just forget about it."

He shoos us out of the kitchen. I gather Sam up; he wants to sleep with the boys, but I think it best for us to stick together. He doesn't fight me. Aunt Carol leads us down the stairs to a room… in the basement. I take a deep breath, swallow down another dose of pride and follow her. At least Sam and Kenny will be right here with me.

I remember there's a door down there. "What if he tries to get in down here?"

"Vernon's gonna sleep out in the living room. He'll be able to hear if anybody's coming." Finally left to ourselves, the boys and I, in silent agreement, crawl into bed exhausted. Who knows what tomorrow's gonna bring. We need to be rested, our minds sharp. We're gonna have to figure something out.

After I begin to hear the rhythmic breathing of the boys' sleep, I have the space to take the situation apart, piece by piece. We aren't going to be able to stay here forever. The boys go back to school on Monday. That gives us tomorrow. They can't be yanked from place to place and learn anything. I have work. Will Mom be home by then? I'm not seeing that as a real possibility with Dad looking to kill her. I'm not gonna be under this roof, in this basement, more than one night. It's too much. I make the decision to go on home and take our chances. I can't deal with any moves from Vernon on top of all this. This is just tempting fate. Surely things will die down a little when Dad sobers up. One can only hope. We need to be in charge of making our own decisions from this point on; to hell with all of them. We have lives, too. Everybody seems to forget that part more often than not. It won't really matter if anyone's there anyway. We're used to doing everything on our own. I try to reassure myself, keep doubt at bay.

What about food? I haven't spent much time in the kitchen, but we can make do. There are recipes, right, and Grandma. It might even be better if all we have to worry about is ourselves. They can do their fighting somewhere else. That is, if they leave us alone.

I wonder if Dad will be at the house. I'm sure he will be in and out, but his search for them ought to keep him occupied. If he knows where we are, we won't be on the priority list. He'll be consumed with Mom and Harold. It isn't about us, right now. We just need to stick together. It's just the three of us now. The game with him won't be much different than it already is. Avoid him. Be quiet. Be invisible.

I finally drift off into a fitful sleep.

I wake up early, the boys still asleep, and tiptoe quietly up the stairs. I wonder if they're up yet. As I near the top step, I begin to hear voices. It's Carol and Vernon, and they're talking about us. I open the door just a crack, so I can hear a little better.

"How long are we going to let them stay?" I hear Carol ask.

"Don't know. Have you heard from Mary this morning?"

They are gossiping over coffee about all this like it is some TV drama or something. Dad didn't shown up here last night; that's one good thing.

"I saw some headlights at about three or so, slowed way down but then drove on by. Not sure if it was him or not. Seems strange for anyone to be out this way, that late."

It sounds like everyday conversation. They seem to be enjoying the excitement a little too much. Suddenly the phone rings. Maybe it's Mom. Who else would call at this hour?

I hear Carol saying, "Yeah, they're here. They were here when we got home. Yeah, they can stay for a while, I guess."

After a long silence, Carol's listening; she warns Mom to be careful and hangs the phone back in its cradle. I hear the click of the plastic. I have to go in. I need more information. I open the door fully, creating some noise. I'm trying to leave the impression of just having arrived on the landing.

"I heard the phone ring," I say, through a yawn, "Did Mom call?"

"They're both all right," Carol says.

I really don't care about him, flashes across my mind.

"I just hung up with her. She and Harold are in a cabin somewhere. Your Dad has been everywhere looking for them. He's leaving threats all over town."

"What about us?" I hear myself saying, "Where does that leave us?"

My voice trails off. The two grown-ups look down at the floor and then there is silence, uncomfortable, awkward silence. I make my excuses and leave the room.

Does anyone care about what happens to us? Are they all just going to stand around and watch as our world falls apart?

We have to get out of here. I shake the boys awake and matter-of-factly say, "We're going home."

"What?" Kenny's the first to respond, rubbing his eyes. It takes him a second to remember where we are and the mess we're in.

"Mom just talked to Carol," I say while shaking my head, "No, I didn't get to talk to her. They don't really want us here, guys. Apparently Dad's been stirring up shit all over town. No one wants to deal with him. They're all afraid...can't really blame them. Let's just go home."

Kenny pipes up, "It is our home."

"But will HE be there?" Sam asks.

"I don't know, Sam. What I do know is that from now on, it's us against them. We're going to start making our own choices. Lord knows we can do a better job than they are, right?" both boys nod in agreement. "What do you think? We're only gonna get one or two more nights here, at the most, anyway. I'd rather take my chances at home."

"Let's do it. Let's just go home," Kenny agrees.

"Okay, get your stuff together. We're gonna sneak out this door down here. Hopefully we can get to the car before anyone catches wind we're leaving."

We make it to the car and get the engine started, "Here we go."

From the rear view mirror, I can see my aunt on the porch waving and yelling for us to come back. It's all for show anyway; it's not like they're going to follow us. Now she can say, "I tried to stop them; they just kept going."

We ride home in complete silence. Each in our own head, wondering what we will find. I take the last curve slowly so we can see if anyone is at the house. The drive is empty. We all breathe a sigh of relief.

Maiden, mother, wise woman

I am haunted by the constant need to remember, but remember what? I don't really want to remember. I just want it all to be erased. I want one of the sides to just not be; it doesn't really matter to me which one. Either me or them. **Erased.** There are worse things than not being born, or dying—carrying around all of these secrets. I'm tired, tired of running, tired of fighting. I need to put them down. How? *Remember. Remember the tools that you were given as a child. Remember the strength you gained. You are a survivor June, not a victim.* Somehow in all of my running I have forgotten. I have forgotten who I am. I have forgotten my beloved Tigua. The slumber has somehow begun to sneak up on me. *Wake up and remember.* I come to the realization with time that remembering my strengths and gifts outweighs the search for the pictures.

How did I survive the war that was my childhood? How was it different from any *real* war? I lived dodging bombs daily, just a different kind. The result was the same—pain, near death. I survived. Can these same tools be used to help me now? Help me let go of their secrets? To find me?

With the aid of the newfound tool of meditation, piece by piece, I begin the process of removing the rubble that I have been buried under. One by one, unlocking the doors to the secrets. Appearing beside each secret stood my strength, my power and my purpose.

You're a survivor June, not a victim.

I'm finally realizing it doesn't matter what the people who claim to be my family do or think. Their movie and what that looks like becomes less important. They can live there, in that out-of-sync place, if they choose. I don't want to. Forgiveness is a funny thing. I've read that true forgiveness comes only when all parties stand fully in the truth and take complete responsiblity for their actions. That rarely happens. It hasn't happened for me. I decide to lay down my sword and walk in a different direction.

No more fighting!

She brings forth opportunities to reinvent oneself...recycle what you think and what you know

We begin the process of bringing order to our lives. We fall into a comfortable routine. It feels good. Good to us. We don't have a dish washer. The dishes, the house, I let go. We keep the animals fed and watered and keep us fed and clean. Homework done, mostly…and work. We do okay, until they show up. Mom and Harold swoop in like they are saving the day, stay a few days. Lots of fancy food, and lots of happy laughter. We want to believe it's real. Then they leave again, or Dad shows up. He's still ranting around, threatening to kill Harold. He has some choice names for him that I will leave unsaid. His obsession keeps him occupied. We live in between.

I still drag the boys up most Sundays for church. We nestle in beside Grandma with thoughts of breakfast rolling around in our heads and bellies. Tradition is breakfast with Grandma. This Sunday I can't get Kenny up, so Sam and I slide in the pew next to Grandma. The music starts, we stand. I hear this familiar velvety voice echo through the church from up in the choir loft. Bob Carney. He's back!

I begin to bump into him everywhere. He's directing the choir now at church. We all join. Before long, the music is taken from church and into our living room. Mom comes home for these nights. Bob's brother plays guitar and has a small band. He has been giving Sam lessons. It's fun to see Sam up there with the grownups making music. Lots of singing lots of dancing. Everything stops when Bob takes over the microphone and that big beautiful voice fills the space. I gravitate to him. Things feel solid around him. Safe.

When he realizes that we are on our own out here, he begins to hang around and help me put the place back in order after our music nights. After awhile he begins to show up early to help us get ready, too. He and I take on that pile of dishes in the kitchen. I let them go for days and even weeks. Bob just dives right in. And…he is so great with Sam; he comes over sometimes in the middle of the day just to play catch in the front yard. I stand at the kitchen window and watch. It makes my heart happy to see Sam having the kind of fun that little boys deserve. An example of what a real man acts like, a good man.

On occasions when Sam has plans, we get to go on real dates. I have a lot to learn from Bob. We only get one fork, where I come from. I am exposed to a life I never knew existed. New experiences, new foods…Chinese food?! I pretend not to be hungry on that date, afraid I might have to use chopsticks, but they bring him a fork! We go to plays and art museums. I break the heel to my fancy shoes the night he takes me to the symphony, I spend the entire evening tip-toeing around.

The music, the places, the culture! I'm learning, always watching. I observe everyone and everything around me.

———oœœo———

Back in the real world...we've been getting phone calls from Harold's wife. She will only talk if Sam answers; Kenny and I just hang up. But poor Sam, the things she says to him about Mom. I don't care if they are true; no little boy needs to hear those sorts of things out loud about his Mom. When we disconnect the phone entirely, she turns it up, on all of us.

Sam's at a sleepover. Bob and I are just getting back from a movie and a late dinner. The headlights hit the house and all the air is pushed from my lungs as if someone hit me in the stomach. There are obscenities written in black spray paint all across the front of our white house. Some of the words I don't even understand. I'm gasping for air. It has to be Harold's wife. We didn't do anything to her, to any of them. We are just here, trying to live. Breathe....

Regaining my composure to some degree, I say, "All of Sam's friends will be passing by in a few hours for church. I can't let them see this. How will he ever show his face at school on Monday? What am I gonna do?"

Bob sees I'm about at the tipping point and takes charge, "Well, does your Dad have some white paint?"

"Are you serious? We can't get it covered up...."

"I think we can get it covered enough. Enough that it won't catch people's attention from the highway."

"It's the whole front; look they even got some on the rock."

"It won't be perfect, June, but it'll be better than this. Now come on; where does Kenny keep the paint?" Bob's urging me to get moving, trying to prevent me from turning into a puddle.

"Down in the barn; he keeps the paint in the barn."

He grabs my hand pulling me in the direction of the door. "What about brushes?"

Once in motion, I begin climbing out of the sinkhole I was falling into, "I'll grab a flashlight. The brushes are in that big closet in the living room, if you want to grab a couple." I look at him, so grateful that he's here with me.

He gives me an encouraging hug. "Now don't worry. We will have it covered up in no time."

Meeting back up front with paint and brushes, we spend the next few hours trying to mask the art work that one of these wonderful adults has left for us.

Dad seems to just show up periodically in the middle of the night these days. I haven't cared enough to ask where he is when he isn't here, lurking. It's creepy to wake to that feeling of being watched. He's just standing in the corner of the room, in the dark, staring. Sam sleeps with a baseball bat. I don't seem to sleep much at all, one eye always open.

Bob has invited me to go to Kentucky with him to visit family. I make arrangements for Sam. We get the whole weekend. I wake up early that morning and there he is, **Dad,** head drooped, sitting at the kitchen table. I try to pretend he's not there. I don't acknowledge him and go about my business of getting myself ready. I packed last night, thank goodness. Less suspicion.

I sneak my suitcase into the hallway just out of view, when I hear Bob's tires on the gravel drive. He knows it's gonna be tricky getting out of here; Dad's truck is out front. I answer the door and he gives me a wink. Steps past me with his hand out.

"Kenny."

Dad pushes back his chair, "Howyadoin'?"

Dad takes a moment noticing my suitcase, looking from my suitcase to Bob then to me. "Where in the hell do you think you're going?"

"We are going to visit Bob's brother," I say, as confidently as possible.

"Where?"

"Kentucky. We will be back Sunday night. Sam is taken care of. He's staying at Carl's for the weekend," I try to hurry and get it all out.

He begins to shake his head no, "You're not going anywhere. Take your suitcase on back to your room now."

Bob jumps in, "Kenny, she's a grown woman. She can go wherever she wants. You have nothing to say about it. You can't stop her. Now, why don't you just sit back down."

Dad starts to protest. Bob says, "Now, I mean it Kenny. We'll be back in a few days."

On that note he grabs my hand, picks up my suitcase in the other, and…we're out. Dad doesn't follow. At that point, I know for sure. He tells Dad to sit down and shut up and gets away with it.

I trust him.

Bob is offered a teaching job in a city a few hours away, at a fancy all girls college. He decides to take it and is planning to move away. I'm not sure how I can live here without him. He has become such an integral part of our lives here. Kenny has even begun to come out of his room sometimes to hang out when Bob's around.

"Now don't worry, June, we can see each other on the weekends. You can come visit me, and I'll be coming back home."

"What about Sam? I can't just leave him here. I'm not gonna be able to get away for a whole weekend," I'm trying to fight the tears that are threatening to spill over.

"Sam's spending more time with your Mom, since your Dad went into rehab, isn't he?"

"Yeah...I guess so."

"It will be fun, June, you'll see. You'll love it there; there's so much to do. So much life with all of the students. People from everywhere. Lots of music, lots of art."

But what about the time in between? What happens here without my rock? My safety again once removed.

Things do seem to be better here with Dad out of the picture, in rehab...hopefully it works. Bob and I do the back and forth thing for a while. The more I'm out of the picture, the more Mom steps back in. Good for Sam. She and Harold ran off and got married... our house is for sale. Time to move on.

Bob asks me to marry him, and I accept. After all this, it's strange for us to be separated, the boys and I, I mean. Sam's gonna live with Mom and Harold. Harold is good to Sam. Kenny is getting his own place. He's decided he's not living with any of them ever again. Never again.

A new chapter, for all of us.

The lotus represents purity of mind and body
along with actions and speech.... It rises above
the muddy waters of attatchment and desire

In my childhood bedroom, gathering the remnants that made up my life, I gently pick up the medicine pouch. Grandma gave it to me so long ago. One by one, I remove my precious treasures. My beloved panther, the tiger, and there's the Teacher. The stone is cold in my fingers. I hold Tigua tight. Remembering. I turn the totem over and over in my hand.

I get the feeling of a presence behind me, so I turn quickly, startled.

"Teacher!" I throw my arms around his neck, "It's been too long."

"The time has come to move forward. Nothing can change as long as you are clinging to the scenery, June. The tide is turning now."

I step back, take a moment, looking at him intently. "I keep having this dream. It's very weird. Bob takes me to the emergency room, because the pain in my arm is so severe. I can't even think. The doctors take a look and decide it needs to come off. Using this laser kind of thing, they amputate. Just like that, no blood or anything. Anyway, leaving the hospital my arm feels exactly the same. Excruciating! I can still feel the pain. Arm or no arm. I looked into it; I think they call it phantom pain. I have the dream most every night."

The Teacher takes me into his arms, "June, the longing will be with you for a long, long time. Stepping away will leave a vacancy, a void where your family should be. These are their choices, June. If you stay, if you go, they are never going to be different. When the time comes that you can stop being an actor in their movie it will all begin unraveling at the seams. It's as if you are being removed from a cult. Brainwashed. The deconstruction of their programming will come in time, with space and separation. It's time to make your own family now. Fill that vacancy with people of your choosing. The circle of family is whomever you choose to love, love without demands in return and without secrets! Don't close your heart, June."

"I'm kind of afraid of people," I tell him.

"You will need to get far, far, away. Trust that the people you need will be sent to you. Your journey is far from over, June, and it's not going to be easy. It's time to break free and begin the process of putting all the pieces in their places. Remember all you have learned. Look back through the events that have created your life and remember. The tools and truths you have gained will prove to be very useful to you in the future. Use them wisely. Don't allow yourself to be taken by the slumber, remember!" he's saying as he begins to fade from sight.

It's hard to swallow past the lump in my throat. This is all I have ever known. I take a moment, look around. I guess I never really believed this day would come. I put the last few things in the car and close the trunk. With a weird mixture of anticipation and reluctance, I get behind the wheel of my metal horse. I start the engine and begin to back out of the drive. Inching my way onto the highway, I hear a familiar voice, the voice of my dear old friend from the other side.

"Don't look back, June," I hear Tigua say. "Don't ever look back."

With that, I take his cue, turn up the radio, and drive.

Destination...LIFE!

Maiden, mother, wise woman

The day Grandma passed away; I lost the last brick of my foundation. The only one I ever had. How can I go on when the only person to ever love me is gone? We moved Grandma in with Mom after her heart attack. The only way to see her was to keep peace with the family.

I get a call from Mom. "June, we have Grandma back home now. We have things set up with hospice. They are saying she doesn't have more than a few weeks left. She's asking for you."

Sundays are our days. I get her all to myself; Mom and Harold get a break. We talk, and she remembers, sharing all of her funny stories. She gets so tickled retelling the story about Dad and the gorilla. She doesn't have to look too far to find funny stories about Dad. She's trying to put the pieces together, too, as if things are gnawing at her. She asks a lot of questions, questions about Dad. Remembering, connecting dots. She just shakes her head. "Not good," she says.

On Wednesday, I get a call, "You had better get down here, June. They say it won't be long now." *Everyone's pretty gentle with me though this time. There's fear that this might be the last straw; I might fall off the edge.*

I quickly cancel my appointments for the rest of the week, throw a few things in a bag and make the journey of goodbyes. Upon entering my Mom's house, the weight in the air is palpable. The matriarch of our family, the glue that has held us together, is fading away. The fragility of our house of cards presents itself clearly to all.

I push my way through Aunt Carol and Uncle John to get back to the room they have set up for Grandma. There she is. She looks so small, so tiny. Her eyes are closed, and she's lying so still. I can't breathe.

She reaches out and takes hold of my hand firmly, "I knew you would come."

She works to speak; in her silence, she has gathered more of the pieces. She's trying to put the puzzle together too. On the other side, we have all the answers. Here in the game it seems it's all about finding them again. Her last few pieces are close, and I hold the key. I make out only fragments, but I can easily fill in the rest. She's muttering about the numerous times I came knocking in the middle of the night. Chi-Chi under one arm.

"Why wouldn't you tell me, June?"

"I don't know Grandma. I was afraid. I just didn't know how."

"I'm sorry. I just didn't know," she shook her head, "I just didn't know."

"Shhh, now Grandma. You knew what I allowed you to see, Grandma. You're my angel. You know that. I wouldn't be here right now if it weren't for all you did for me. You did your job well, you gave me what I needed, love. You quit worrying about me now. This is your time. I love you so much." With that, she closes her eyes, seeming to rest peacefully. I run from the room to the back door.

The coughing has started. I can't breathe. I need some air. Mom follows me out.

"I can't be here. I can't do this," I make a dash for my car. I drive and I drive. I find a place to stay for the night. I need to be alone, to think. How am I going to exist without her? Will I ever come back here?

After a long sleepless night, I decide I have to go back. Not for them, but for her. She has given me so much. It's time to be there for her, now. No one seems surprised to see me. Back in her room, she says the only words she has uttered since I left: "I knew you'd come back."

"She's been waiting for you," Mom says.

The stream of people never seem to stop. So many people. Bob shows up with our two girls. We have been lucky enough to spend some fabulous time with Grandma through the years. She has stayed with us for months at a time. More coughing. Can't breathe.

I get Bob off to the side, "You are going to have to be there for the girls," I tell him. "I can't do this. I have nothing to give them; they're gonna need you," he holds me in a loving embrace.

My cousin and I decide to take the shift through the night. Everyone is asleep. It's as if we're in some sort of void, just the three of us. He's reading the Bible to her softly. I again find my spot, curling in beside her, remembering those long ago years—the stories, the feelings of safety, all laced with so much love. Whenever he took a needed break, I quietly tell her how loved she is, how much I love her.

"I love you so much, Grandma. I'm gonna be okay. It's okay to be tired, Grandma. You have done so many wonderful things for so many people. You have worked so hard. Go on home now. God is calling you."

The next morning, early, Mom sends me down to get some rest. She promises to call me if there are any changes. My cousin has gone home to get some sleep. Aunt Carol's asleep in the basement, Uncle John in the living room. I no sooner get settled in when I hear Mom call my name. I take the stairs two at a time. Mom's lying beside Grandma, cradling her head in her arms, stroking her face. She is singing Amazing Grace, Grandmas favorite, softly. Aunt Carol is close behind me; Uncle John has already taken his place. He moves over to make room. We join in the singing. She breathes her last breath. We come together as one in our love for her, at least for a moment.

Now the hole is bigger—the void, the vacancy where family goes. I have to just keep moving, have to keep moving. It threatens to swallow me. I have no one. She was the only incentive to keep up the charade, the pretense of family, of mother and daughter.

Remember!

A limb of the tree has fallen, but it has sprouted new roots. A small tree is beginning to grow, a healthy tree with no secrets.

Remember!

A tree where the roots begin with me and Bob, and our girls.

Japanese word meaning circle.... Enzo symbolizes absolute enlightenment, strength and elegance, along with the universe and the void

I find myself back at the beginning. I meander towards my new spot. My longtime companion and protector, Sadie, is stopped on the path up ahead, waiting impatiently for me to catch up. When I finally reach her, she falls in beside me...for a second. It's a beautiful morning; the air is crisp in my lungs. The animals are resurfacing after their long winter slumber. The birds are fluttering. The sun light filters through the newly sprouting leaves, a welcome contrast to the gray and dreary days of fading winter. Sadie darts off for a game of chase with a squirrel. She bounces through the underbrush of the woods lining the path in search of her opponent. Her bounce reminds me of the feeling of flying over the creek with Ginger. A smile brushes my lips at the thought of my dear old friend. We are getting close, "Come on Sadie Bird. The river is up ahead," I call out. She bounds back and fills time by running circles around me as I walk. "It's right up here," I tell her laughing. She looks up at me tongue hanging out, "Oh, go on. I'll meet you up there." She takes off leading the way to my cliff.

It's not the same cliff; its a new one. I found this spot, a place where I can think; try to fit the pieces of my life together. Faintly, in the far recesses of my mind, I hear...*Remember!* That same soft familiar voice from long ago...*Remember what you know.* The voice gets a little stronger as I focus in on it...*Remember your medicine pouch, June. Remember what you know.* I'm more than a little startled; I haven't heard that voice for a really long time. Sifting through my purse, I find the small pouch from childhood. My medicine pouch. I remove the small stone totems. I take a moment with each, remembering. I haven't had them out since I left home. I set each out on the ground before me and the memories begin to swirl. I didn't realize how much I missed each of them. I take a moment with the little carving of the lady with the red scarf. I miss Grandma. Remember!

I wonder if I can still get there. I wonder if they will still be there. Looking out over the tree tops I can hear the soothing sounds of the running water below...*Remember.*

"The water of life," the Teacher once said. "You came here through the water of life." Glancing down, I notice a large buck at the water's edge. Feeling my presence, he turns his noble head up to meet my gaze. I can feel him, his strength and his peace. The memories begin to flood in. All of our grand adventures, the rainbow bridge, the Teacher. My haven of safety. I think until the words run dry, my mind still, very calm. I slip gently to the other side. Just like old times. Looking around, I notice that things haven't changed much. I'm deposited right in the meadow, just like when I was a kid. Up ahead on the path, in all his glory, is Tigua. My heart jumps. My legs start moving as if they have a mind of their own; we cover the distance that separates us quickly. I throw my arms around his neck and snuggle my face down in his soft blue-black fur.

Tigua purrs softly.

After a moment, he says, "Stand back now, June, I want to get a good long look at you. It's been awhile."

I pipe in, "It's been forever. I didn't know if I could come," I say, looking down at the length of myself, "as a grown up."

"And that you are; I would say you have done quite well, sweet June, you have grown up to be quite a beautiful woman."

"I thought maybe it was all just my imagination. The doctors thought I made it all up, made you up...." My voice is trailing off. I take a good look around. It feels good to be here, "I heard you calling my name when I was back on the cliff."

"That's why we called you here today, June. After all the battles we have fought, we don't want you to fall into the slumber."

"The slumber?" I ask.

"The grownups down there seem to fall into some sort of slumber. They forget; they forget the magic. They forget to play, and laugh. We need you to stay awake, to not get lulled in. As for being a grown up, know that you can come here anytime; age doesn't matter. This is God's country. Come on, let's take a walk," I fall in beside him, and we begin to make our way down the familiar path.

"Where are we going?"

"Some things never change," Tigua chuckles. "Always with the questions. Everyone is gathered in the village. We have been waiting a long time for you to remember."

With that I fall into an unaccustomed silence as I soak in the familiar surroundings—the meadow with wild flowers of all colors. But the poppies, Grandma's flower, majestically rise above it all. The trees are just up ahead.

Entering the woods, I begin to hear the familiar rustling of the animals and flowing water in the distance. As the waterfall comes into view, it takes my breath away. It is beautiful, so many shades of green. At the river's edge, meeting my gaze is a magnificent elk. His beautiful rack dips into a graceful bow before returning to the pleasures of the water. Up ahead, as if appearing out of nowhere, is the bridge. The dense heavy light of the colors seemingly join the earth on either side of the river. *It only appears for those who are called.* The tingling starts with my toes as my foot touches the bridge, as if the light were circulating through my body. I have never really stepped on it before. I've always had a ride. Today, I am walking in on my own. I stand a little taller. I reach over and touch my friend.

"I have missed you, Tigua. I have missed this," I spread my arms out wide, "The peace. It's been lonely down there. I'm sick all the time. The doctors have labeled me with all these disorders. No one seems to understand. They all think I'm crazy. But I don't."

"You are not crazy, June. You just know. They have all forgotten," Tigua replies.

Arriving on solid ground, we are met by the lady with the flowing red scarf. I break into a run and wrap my arms around the woman's neck.

"Grandma," I cry, tears stream freely down my face.

"Shhh…. There, there, Junebug."

"I have missed you so much," I say between sobs. "It's so hard to live down there without you, Grandma."

"Shhh…now. We have some celebrating to do. We have our little Junebug back. We thought you would never come. It's been too long," the woman croons. "Let's join the others." We meander on down the path to the village. I can't keep my hands off of either of them. Their touch feels so good, brings back so many good memories. I've spent a lot of time lately with the bad ones. Freedom!

Coming up to the edge of the village, I see everyone is gathered. They are all here, the Teacher, the Seer, Mahala. Grandma and Tigua are at my side. Oh, there's Zuni, and the noble Paint mare. And…

Ginger! I can't contain myself; I dash to her first, throwing my arms around her neck.

"I have missed you so much, all of you," hugs all around. After the greetings are over, the flap to the Seer's tent is lifted. The familiar scent of sage is wafting from the opening, the accustomed fire in the center. Everyone takes a seat forming the circle, Tigua on one side, between me and the Seer, Grandma on the other. The Seer rises, taking the floor. The murmurs around the room quiet; I can hear a pin drop. He begins to speak.

"June, we have called you here today to help you remember. It's time for you to put the last of the pieces together. You have things to do. It's time to remember."

I can feel the nerves building in my belly, not sure I want to remember, but I have the burning need. With that, the cup is raised to his lips and passed on to the Teacher. One by one, the cup is raised, and now it is my turn. Lifting the cup with a familiar twinge, I remember my distaste of the liquid as a child. A smile crosses as the potion slides down gently. From the ground at his side, the Seer takes the grand pipe into his hands. Holding it high, he chants for the gods to show me all that I need to see. Lowering the pipe, he takes a draw. The pipe makes its way around the circle. As smoke fills my lungs, I close my eyes, enjoying the soft tingly feeling that begins to move through my body.

The Seer brings me back by saying, "June, today we are going to see your life. Pay close attention. Look objectively and see. Watch through the eyes of a survivor. You have fought and won many battles. Your strength and courage have set the stage for all of the change. See in between the lines. Learn and remember. It's time for you now."

With that, it's as if I'm watching a movie. The horror of my childhood plays out in front of my eyes. The bath tub. Flowing with the water and meeting Tigua for the first time. Dad and his lurking, slipping in and out of my bedroom. The gorilla—I can feel myself smiling. That was a good moment. The trailer. The basement. All the ugliness, it is all there. But watching from here, there is a balance. I had so much fun coming here. Such warmth and love here. And Grandma, there she is with me on her heels. I watch it all play out. It is as if I can watch both places at the same time. I can see the parts I missed while coming here. They aren't a shock somehow. Dad in my bed. I knew, I just couldn't see. Somehow, having the pictures fills a vacancy, a place where doubt seems to lurk.

In *their* picture, the picture down there, nothing ever really happened to me. According to them I had a perfect childhood. *Just forget about it.* So many fun times. I never could understand. Were we living in two separate movies? *Forgive and forget.* I guess as long as the masks are kept on they can keep up the charade. Nicely decorated homes, pretty clothes. Just keep the mask in place. Mine has been slipping lately. I can't seem to play both roles anymore.

As I watch, a strength begins building inside. I am a survivor. Some want me to be a victim; others want me to pretend that I made it all up. Watching, I am able to see what was. The veils fall away. I have a feeling of pride growing as I watch the little girl maneuver all of those horrible situations. She figured out how to come here. She survived. As the pictures begin to fade from view I can feel myself coming back to the present, feeling different somehow. Everything has a different clarity, is a little sharper around the edges, more whole somehow. The Seer touches my shoulder gently.

"You are a courageous warrior, June, with the truth as your weapon. This is your movie, your life. You are the director; don't make the same mistake and become invisible. Make your movie with thought, conviction, and integrity. It's time to be You. Become who you were intended to be. Stand tall in your experiences and shout them to the world. They need to know. The world needs to wake up. Children come into the world in ultimate purity as gifts to their parents. Protection and safety is their God given right. So often, these precious gifts are thrown away. Your girls are the first women in your lineage to experience a childhood without suffering, without a daddy sneaking into their rooms at night. You broke away June. You broke the cycle. You gave all those coming after, the gift of freedom."

With that he rises and the rest begin to follow. We are led by the Teacher down to the river and gather around the base of the rainbow.

The Teacher begins speaking, "June, the healing waters of Rainbow Bridge are before you."

Taking my hand, he leads me under the base of the bridge. The others form part of a circle from river's edge to river's edge, the Teacher and I in the center. I am facing him, both hands in his grasp.

He looks into my eyes intently and says softly, "Upon entering the water, all will be washed clean, all pain, all suffering. With the water, you will find balance and clarity. Freedom from the past."

With these words, he guides me into the water. I can feel the coolness inching its way up my legs with each step. The current is flowing against my body, tugging at my dress. The doors to the many secrets seemingly pushed open with the power of the water. With their release, the dawning, the realization...THEY AREN'T MY SECRETS! They can have them back. Guard them themselves. I'm off duty.

I take a deep breath before the final step takes me under. Submerged, I can feel the water circulating around me, as if going inside and cleaning out every crevice. A beam of light at the surface catches my attention. I'm drawn like a moth. As I burst through the surface, I can feel the warmth from the light on my face, pouring into my body. I look around, one at a time; women begin to erupt through the surface of the water. First one, then two. In the end hundreds emerge, as if catching their breath after being held under far too long. Freedom!

Beckoned ashore by the Teacher, I work to regain my composure. I feel as light as air. The weight I've carried for so long has been washed away with the current. Doors open! Secrets out! Light flows through the dark, dank rooms that are hidden deep inside. A sparkle of deep peace enters my heart. The Teacher reaches for my hand to guide me from the water. Here in the center of the circle, all of my loved ones are gathered around, the Teacher begins to stroke my hand.

"It's time to go back to the world and tell them what you have learned, June. You have a strong voice and pure heart. There are so many others. Wounded and broken. Bring out the survivor in them. Show them what they are missing. Help them to be free. Your light and truths can guide many out of the darkness. Help them awaken from their slumber. Don't forget, June. Remember, always remember! Be vigilant of the slumber. Through the stillness of your mind, you will keep your peace and your clarity."

With that, I begin to feel my eyes getting heavy. I remember the familiar signal. There I am perched on my cliff, the water flowing below, Sadie standing guard over our spot. The big buck still gazing up in my direction, as if time stood still. That strange feeling of wonder tingles in my chest.

I see my totems on the ground before me. One by one, I return them lovingly to my worn and tattered medicine pouch. The panther

I hold tight for a second, remembering the vibrancy emanating from him, his coat shining. My dear, dear friend and protector. Faintly, as if way off in the distance, I can hear.

"I am always with you, June. Always watching. *Remember…Remember…Remember!*"

CPSIA information can be obtained at www.ICGtesting.com
Printed in the USA
LVOW06s0708180713

343384LV00002B/69/P